W9-AXW-824

The ·PEACE· Child

The ·PEACE· Child

Ann Phillips

Oxford University Press
Oxford Toronto Melbourne

Oxford University Press, Walton Street, Oxford OX2 6DP

Oxford New York Toronto
Delhi Bombay Calcutta Madras Karachi
Petaling Jaya Singapore Hong Kong Tokyo
Nairobi Dar es Salaam Cape Town
Melbourne Auckland

and associated companies in
Beirut Berlin Ibadan Nicosia

Oxford is a trade mark of Oxford University Press

First published 1988

British Library Cataloguing in Publication Data

Phillips, Ann, *1930–*
The peace child.
I. Title
823'.914[J] PZ7

ISBN 0-19-271560-7

Set by Graphicraft Typesetters Limited, Hong Kong
Printed in Hong Kong

The Families in the Book

The Family at Lordship Butlers

Sir Steven (grandfather)
Hugh (Sir Steven's elder son)
Ede (Hugh's wife)

The Children:

Nicholas
Sisely
Gilbert
Julian (Juliana)
Walter
Maud
Alys
Rose

Servants:

Ursel
Moll
Daw
Kate
Jillot
Austin

The Family at Butlers' Spinney

Richard (Sir Steven's younger son)
Joan (Richard's wife)

The Children:

Avery
Jordan
Pentecost
Adam
Joan

The Castells at East Hatley

Sir Philip
Sir Philip's sons from his first marriage:
Harry
Robert
Annis (Sir Philip's second wife)

The Children:

Christina
Annora
Jossey
Humfrey
Edward

Servants:

Master and Mistress Cheeseman
Hob

Servants at Ship House:

Master Arkwright
Hubbard
Mitchell Harding
Mabell

A drawn sword lay on the table, with its point towards Alys. Alys looked at it and shivered, not only with cold.

There were ten of the family around the table in the high, dark room. Their emotions seemed to Alys to vibrate in the air just as the light from the many candles shimmered and shook. There seemed to be anger there, and grief; but was she the only one who was afraid?

The people around the table were all dark, except for Alys. Dark hair, dark eyes, thick dark eyebrows; and the sun-browned skins of summer and out-of-doors. Only Alys, the youngest one there, was pale. In the candlelight her hair shone somewhere between silver and the palest gold (by day it was the colour of ivory), and her dress was white. The family were called the Black Butlers, because of their dominant colouring. For a moment the old wonder distracted Alys's mind, as she looked around at them: how did it happen, this single white chick in a farmyard? Her brothers had teased her incessantly until her grandfather, Sir Steven, had stopped them; but the old nickname, Lilyflower, had stuck.

'Stand there, Lilyflower,' said Sir Steven, almost as if he were echoing her thoughts. 'Stay by me. Can everyone see Alys?'

He pulled her close to the side of his high-backed chair. Her father, Hugh, drew his stool a little closer to Alys on the other side.

'What have I done?' asked Alys, looking from Sir Steven to the sword. She was alarmed that she had made some appalling blunder and this family council was to call her to account for it. Summoned after midnight; dragged naked out of bed and hurriedly dressed by her sisters; brought down here by her mother while they were forbidden to come — the only girl of the family present in a gathering of men: her crime must be indescribable. It couldn't be anything this time to do with her spitfire temper and her notorious lack of proper little-girl meekness. It must be something worse.

At least, her mother was there. 'What have I done?' Alys repeated, this time directly to Ede Butler.

'Nothing,' said her mother. 'It's no fault of yours, Alys. Be quiet now and stand there. Avery is dead.'

'Dead how?' asked Alys, trying to take it in. Avery was the eldest and her favourite of her Butler cousins, who lived close by where a spinney grew beside a deep, narrow brook. Avery was the laughing, singing, strong-armed young man (a year older than her eldest brother, Nicholas) who led the fun when they all raced their ponies over the commons or the stubbles, who had taught Alys to shoot with a bow and to fly a hawk. How could Avery be dead?

'Drowned,' said her mother.

'Where is he, then?' asked Alys.

'In Cantebridge, where he died,' said her father. 'He must stay there until the coroner and his jury have met. Tomorrow, please God.'

'What has it got to do with me — why am I here, and not the other girls?' Alys persisted.

'Be quiet, child,' said Sir Steven, so seriously that this time Alys obeyed. She was beginning to understand, as if a picture shifted and came into focus, why when she and her mother came into the long room all the men had been kneeling at their prayers before the crucifix on the wall; and why upstairs Sisely, her eldest sister, had been helpless with tears while the others, Julian and Maud and Rose, had hunted in a frantic hurry for Alys's dress and her plaited belt and a comb for her hair. Nobody had found her shoes, and now she burrowed bare feet into the straw which covered the floor. She was pleased when one of the dogs, old Kemp, lay down by her, half-covering her ankles, and produced a little warmth.

Looking around the table again, she understood more of the strength of feeling she could sense. Uncle Richard, Avery's father, sat white and heavy-eyed, a man in shock; his two other sons, Jordan and Adam (her clever cousins, one to be a lawyer and one to be a priest) were still and silent, mourning Avery. Avery's mother wasn't there; Alys pictured her over at Butlers' Spinney in a frenzy of grief, as lost as Sisely. But her own brothers, Nicholas and Gilbert and Walter, were tense with some emotion — anger, surely? But why? And what had it all to do with herself? 'Nothing' made no sense. Nobody had sent for Maud or Rose and bundled them into a white dress. Neither Maud nor Rose had got one.

She had known all along that she was different from the other children; and the white dress was part of it. She wasn't allowed to wear it — she ran about like the other little girls in frocks of homespun brown or grey, with a blue linen overdress for best. But all the time it was there, looped over a clothes-rail; and at times it was fetched down and altered by her mother or Sisely so that it still fitted her. The fit now was none too good — it was long enough, but tight under the arms. She fidgeted a bit and Sir Steven put a hand on her sleeve, drawing the attention of all the Butlers to her.

'Look well at Alys, kinsmen,' he said. 'And look at the sword, and where it points, remembering what she is. Are you fit, Richard? Shall we begin?'

Uncle Richard made a noise in his throat. Ede Butler pushed a mug of warm ale towards him. 'Drink,' she said to him, gentle, and he did, moving stiffly like a puppet.

'Begin, sir,' said Jordan, speaking for him. 'We are well enough.' But Jordan himself was shivering, and his teeth chattered if he didn't clench them.

'Who found Avery?' Sir Steven asked.

'I did,' said Nicholas gruffly. 'Jordan and I.'

'Tell us what happened,' said Sir Steven.

'We went to Cantebridge,' said Nicholas. 'To the Midsummer Fair. Avery said we should go. He and

Jordan went last year, and I wanted to see it too. Everyone goes.'

'You should have asked,' said Hugh Butler, but not sounding very angry.

'Yes, sir,' said Nicholas. 'It was Avery, Jordan, Gilbert and I. I took Sisely — my mother said she could spare her — and Avery took Pentecost up behind him.' Pentecost was Avery's sister. Alys pictured the cheerful little party, the two girls riding behind their handsome brothers, Jordan and Gilbert on ponies, larking as they rode.

'When the best of the fair was over for the day, we went to the ale-house on the Greencroft for a meal,' said Nicholas. 'It was so full that we took our pies and a jug of ale and found a quiet place on the river-bank. When the ale ran out, Avery picked up the jug and went for more. It was dark by then. He didn't come back. When we got tired of waiting, Jordan and I went calling him. He wasn't in the ale-house or the privy. We got lanterns — it was black dark — and we saw him floating in the river, caught against a boat moored by the bank. Jordan went in for him, but he was dead when we got him on the bank.'

Alys moved, distressed at the thought of it. Her father took her hand and held it.

'Is there more?' said grandfather.

'Of course there's more,' exploded Gilbert and Jordan said, 'Go on.'

'Yes,' said Nicholas. 'The other thing is that Harry Brag was in Cantebridge. And his beloved brother Robert. They were at the fair — most of us saw them. We kept well out of their way; but Robert spoke to Pentecost.'

'Pinched her cheek,' said Gilbert. 'And called her coney.'

'He would,' said Hugh Butler. He frowned; but Alys could see no great harm in a man's calling a girl by a pet name (even if it did mean 'rabbit').

'Who's Harry Brag?' she couldn't resist asking.

Ede shushed her, but Gilbert was already answering. 'One of the Castells — our enemies,' he said. 'The one who stole Avery's horse, last year. Broad as a barn and wicked as Old Harry himself.'

'Don't name the devil in this house,' said Ede, 'and don't speak of enemies. We have no enemies.'

'They were in the ale-house when we went in there first,' said Jordan. 'It was one reason we left. But they'd gone when we went back looking for Avery.'

'And out of this,' said grandfather flatly, 'you build a fairy-tale that Harry Castell and Robert Castell drowned Avery in the river. Is that it?'

'It can't have been an accident,' said Nicholas, almost shouting. 'Now can it, sir? Avery knew the river-bank; he had only drunk a cup or two. And if he did fall in, what then? Avery could swim.'

'Tripped in the dark,' suggested Hugh. 'Stunned himself falling.'

'There will be the inquest,' said Jordan, looking up. 'The coroner's jury will look to see whether there are any marks on Avery — of a blow, or strangling. We must wait for the law.'

'I wait for no law!' said Nicholas, banging the table. 'It isn't a silly squabble about a horse, this time. A man has been killed — one of us. Our enemies were there —'

'And nothing can be proved against them,' said Uncle Richard, wearily.

'And they're sitting there in Hatley, only a few miles away, laughing up their sleeves, as like as not,' Gilbert added, as hot as Nicholas.

'Do you or do you not want a blood-feud, Nicholas, Gilbert?' said grandfather. 'I and your grandmother chose against it, when she lived — she was the best Christian of us all. So did Matthew and Margery Castell. Our children agreed with us, and Alys is the living proof of that agreement.'

'Alys is my child — mine and Ede's,' said Hugh Butler softly Ede looked at him as if she were grateful; but Alys wondered why he was telling people what they already knew.

'And what would you do — rush off to Hatley with your swords drawn, and murder women and children in their beds?' demanded Sir Steven. 'If Harry and Robert are guilty, you can count upon it they'll be gone from there by now.'

'We can't not fight, grandfather,' protested Gilbert, and Walter nodded vigorously. He was only twelve, and had only just scraped into this council; but he sat flushed and fierce-eyed. Like Gilbert, he thought mainly of war: he and Gilbert were training themselves to go as archers to the fighting in France. (Sir Steven raised his eyebrows at this idea, and believed they would grow out of it.)

'Who knows what they'll do next?' Nicholas asked vehemently. 'Last year it was Avery's horse; and now Avery.'

'That's supposition,' said Hugh; and Nicholas glowered.

'I repeat, peace is our only choice,' said grandfather. 'The sword points at Alys. You know who she is. Look at her.'

'So there she stands!' exclaimed Nicholas. 'And this sort of peace, a knuckling-under to thieves and murderers, is fitter for children than for men. If that's the purpose of having her here, some of us would rather she were gone.'

'You've said enough, Nicholas,' Ede Butler broke in. 'I don't care for truckling to braggarts either, but if any unhappiness came to Alys through you — I wouldn't have you under my roof. Now then! Whatever happens between us and the Castells, Alys is not to blame.'

'I beg your pardon,' said Nicholas, suddenly calmer. 'I don't want harm to come to her, madam. But I've heard all this before —'

So have I, thought Alys. It was beginning to sound like so many family quarrels, half heard and three quarters forgotten. She scrambled on to her father's knee and fell asleep against his shoulder.

When she woke the candles were out and the shutters were open to the bleak light of early morning. The room seemed full of sleepers — her brothers, who slept in the main hall, had unrolled their mattresses and were stretched out on the floor; Adam slept with his head on the table. Grandfather was gone, and his sword with him. Her mother and father were talking quietly to Richard Butler and Jordan, who stood at the passage door.

'It's time you told Alys,' said Jordan softly. 'The questions she's asking now ought to be answered. How old is she — nine? Nearly ten? She's not a fool. You ought to talk to her.'

'It seems soon to break up her world,' whispered Ede.

'Better you than Harry Brag,' said Richard harshly.

He and Jordan shook Adam awake, and the cold air that came in at the door as it opened to let them out cleared the last shreds of Alys's sleep.

'Are we having a war with the Castells?' she said; and her father, who still held her in his arms, looked down at her. 'No, no,' he said. 'No blood-feuds. This time again the old heads prevailed. But as the old heads get weaker, and the young heads get stronger, what will become of our precious peace?'

'What has it got to do with me?' said Alys, as her father set her on her feet.

'Nothing,' said her mother. 'I'm taking you back to bed.'

But Jordan's words came back to her as she crawled into the bed she shared with Maud and Rose, and settled back to sleep. 'It's time you told Alys . . . Talk to her.'

The family from Lordship Butlers, which was what people called the farm where Sir Steven and Hugh and his children lived, went over to the spinney to see Avery where he lay dead and to say prayers over him. The coroner's court had judged his death to be an accident, to Nicholas's and Gilbert's disgust, and he had been brought home to be buried. The Butlers' Spinney house was built as a little tower, and it had its own tiny chapel tucked away up a short flight of steps. Avery lay there, with five candles at his head and feet, and a black cloth spread over him to the shoulders. Alys thought he looked very wise, as if he knew everything now.

After his burial, things gradually went back to a look of the normal in Alys's world. The Butlers were all too busy, especially in the summer, to be able to brood over troubles, though a tension still underlay their everyday lives. Even Sisely, by concentrating fiercely on the work Ede gave her to do, showed a face of composure to the world; but she found no spark of pleasure in what she did. Just occasionally her grief flashed out, as once when she shook Maud for teasing Walter. Although Walter was only twelve his passionate love for his cousin Pentecost was the joke and scandal of the village. Scandal because he carved her name on trees, and was always staring at her in church instead of saying his prayers; joke because she was two years older than he and thought to be no beauty — the blackest of all the Black Butlers, with straight thick sooty hair and eyebrows that met above her nose.

'Let him be!' shrieked Sisely, rocking Maud on her heels. 'Love is no joke.'

'Well, but he can't marry her, Sis,' said Maud. 'Uncle

Richard wants her to marry one of Aunt Joan's rich friends. Of course it's a joke.'

Sisely slapped her, burst into tears, and ran out of doors. Maud sulked, knowing the quarrel was her fault. 'Sisely's always cross these days,' she said.

'You know why,' said Walter. 'Father wants her to get married, now she's sixteen, and she's been promised for three years. But she only liked Avery, and he's dead. It's no wonder that she's cross.'

'She ought to honour and obey,' said Maud in a righteous manner. 'When I'm old enough I shall marry whoever father tells me to.'

'I shan't,' said Alys, putting down her distaff and thread. 'I shall scream, and fight, and starve myself, and make them let me marry my true love.'

'You would,' said Walter unkindly (he was still upset), 'and make everybody wretched before you were through. We all know your terrible temper. You're a fine peace —'

He stopped himself abruptly and turned poppy-red.

'Peace what? What, what?' demanded Alys.

'Piece of trouble, I was going to say,' Walter finished unconvincingly.

'You weren't — it sounded different,' insisted Alys.

'Peace-maker, he meant,' said Julian from where she sat quietly sewing. 'Like the bad wife in the song:

How hey, it is none lease,
I dare not seyn when she saith Peace!'

(which means, 'Hey hey, it's God's own truth, I don't dare speak when she says Shush!')

The song had been Avery's favourite, and everybody sat quiet for a moment remembering Avery, on his tall horse, coming singing home.

The quarrel was over, but Walter's words had deepened Alys's sense of a mystery surrounding herself. She put aside her spinning and went upstairs and took her mother's mirror — a round of polished silver — from where it was kept hidden in case it should tempt the girls to vanity. She brooded over her pale face and almost colourless hair.

'It's something hidden from me,' she said aloud. 'I don't look like the others. I've got a white dress. I have to stand with a sword pointing at me, and grandfather says "Look at her". Walter knows something he tries to cover up, and I think Julian does too. Jordan says I should be told. And I want to know. All right then, Alys Butler. You want to know — find out.'

She went like a person compelled, absorbed in her mission, down the stairs of the house (which were outside it and took her into bright sun) and away over the fields to Emm's house.

Red-headed Emm was the young sister of Ursel, who worked at Lordship Butlers, and Alys's particular friend. The friendship flourished in spite of the fact that the two girls, much of an age, lived entirely different lives: Alys as a landowners' daughter, although not a rich one; Emm as a villein or peasant girl, whose family all had to work for their living from a very early age — especially as their father had died young. Emma, Emm's mother, was the village baker and Emm and her young brother Batt were watching the big oven in the bakehouse when Alys arrived. They had shovels for fetching loaves in and out, and were both pink in the face.

'Emm,' said Alys, pulling her aside. 'Leave that — Batt can manage. Tell me, do you know anything secret about me?'

'Not a thing,' said Emm. 'Are you gone soft in the head, Alys Butler?'

'No, but — ' said Alys. 'You see, Emm, I'm not a Black Butler, am I?'

'Not you,' said Emm. 'You were boiled too long.'

'Well then, I'm somebody else, aren't I?' said Alys. 'I might be anybody. A lost princess.'

Emm laughed heartily. 'I never heard tell that the old king lost a princess,' she said. 'If he had, you can be sure he'd have come here to look for her first. "Where can she be," he'd have said. "Why, in God's name, she must be in Harlton! I'll try Lordship Butlers." And the new king's a sight too young to have lost any daughters yet — supposing he had any.'

This was certainly true. The young Richard II was only thirteen.

'You can laugh,' said Alys. 'But I still think something odd happened to me. When I was a baby, I expect.'

'You can't hardly expect me to remember when you were a baby, Lys,' said Emm. 'When you were born, I was only a few months old myself. Try my mother — she's inside, working the dough.'

Old Emma (who was not old, but so-called to keep her distinct from her daughter) was up to her elbows in the dough, but could still spare a minute for a gossip.

'What's that, my duck?' she said. 'Remember you as a babe? Of course I do — a little pale creature, even then.'

'Was there anything odd about me? Different?' Alys begged. 'Any stories?'

Emma paused in her kneading, and straightened her back.

'Stories,' she said. 'That makes me think. It's not a story, but ... When you were born, Alys, for a few days the word was that you were a boy. All round the village it was said, "Ede Butler's got another son." Then we were all told different — "Our mistake, friends — it's a daughter." There was a good laugh in the ale-house, you can imagine. "Don't they Butlers know a boy from a girl," people said.'

'Oh,' said Alys. 'Is that all?'

'That's all,' said Emma; but Alys felt it was a start.

It was quite clear to Alys that Maud didn't know any secret about her: Maud and Alys lived too much in each other's pockets for there to be secrets between them. She decided to tackle Walter. She lay in wait for him one day when he left the priest's house, where he and Adam from the spinney went for lessons every day. Several boys went to Sir William Tele for a short time, to learn to read and write and add up. Walter and Adam had stayed on, and were learning Latin.

When Adam turned aside to go to the spinney, Alys came out from behind a hawthorn bush and joined Walter on the field path. She had brought a pasty for him as bait.

'How was school?' she said. 'Wat, I wish I could go.'

'Don't be daft,' said Walter. 'Girls don't need book-learning.'

'Neither do you, if you're going to be a soldier,' said Alys.

'I'll be too old for soldiering one day,' said Walter. 'Like grandfather, with his stiff leg. Then I may need to read and write.'

'I want to learn,' said Alys restlessly. 'I wish you'd teach me.'

'Girls need to know household things, and mother teaches you,' said Walter. 'You'll never need to read and write.'

'How do you know?' said Alys. 'Walter, I want to know who I am.'

Walter stopped dead on the footpath, his mouthful unchewed. 'Who's been talking to you?' he said. And then more cautiously, 'What do you mean?'

'Don't act innocent,' said Alys. 'I'm not a Black Butler, am I? That's what I mean.'

'Of course you are,' said Walter strenuously. 'What nonsense, Lys.'

'Oh, Wat, do say,' Alys pleaded. 'It's not fair that I'm not told. Please, Wat. I'd tell you if I knew a secret about you. Truly I would.'

Walter weakened a little. 'Look, I'm not allowed to say anything,' he whispered. 'I wasn't meant to know, but I overheard some talk. Father made me promise not to repeat it, and I won't. Everyone at home who knows has promised. So my advice is — ask somewhere else. Where they know, but may not have promised. See?'

Alys didn't see. 'Where, then?' she demanded.

'Honest, I can't say any more,' said Walter. 'All I can do is swear I won't tell anyone you asked — or you'd be in trouble up to your neck.'

'But do just give me a clue, Wat,' said Alys. 'About where to ask.'

'Look over your shoulder,' said Walter, and ran off full pelt down the path.

Alys looked over her shoulder, and saw through the hawthorns of the spinney a small squat tower. Thinking, she followed Walter home.

Out of the Butlers at Butlers' Spinney, Uncle Richard and Aunt Joan would certainly not talk. Jordan had gone back to his studies in London after Avery's funeral, between hay harvest and corn harvest. Adam the would-be priest would probably not talk; and if he didn't talk, he would tell on her. Adam was strict in his principles. Young Joan, who was Maud's age, might not know. After a few days, Alys sought out Pentecost.

The tower-house was built on the edge of the spinney, near a pool of water which the dragon-flies loved. To reach it from Lordship Butlers you had to pass Uncle Richard's hives. Bees are irritable creatures, as everyone knows, and Alys spoke politely to them in passing.

'Fierce fighting ladies, with short swords — don't stab me,' she recited — a charm Jordan had taught her years ago. 'I've come from Lordship Butlers to see Pentecost. Let me pass.'

The bees rustled and buzzed inside and around the hives, but none attacked Alys.

The other hazard was the mud where the cattle had trodden; the edge of the spinney where they had jostled to get to the pool was mashed by their hooves. The causeway, semi-paved with rubble and flints, was a long way round, so Alys hopped from tussock to tussock, holding up her skirt. When she got to the house she took a dipper of water from the rain-water butt at the back door and washed her bare feet. In the summer she liked to leave off her stockings and her heavy shoes, and run free like Emm — though she was likely to get slapped for it if she was caught.

The ground floor of the tower was used for stores and for stalls for horses and cattle. To get to the hall, the main living-room of the house, you went up outside stairs. The hall door was open today; Alys called her name and went in.

The hall of Butlers' Spinney occupied the whole of the first floor of the tower. It was light and beautiful and contained, as well as seats and the dining-table, the loom where Aunt Joan, Pentecost and little Joan wove wool and fine linen. Aunt Joan was a rich woman, and when Uncle Richard had married her, a young widow, she had brought him houses and land on the Kent-Sussex border. But she still spun and wove all the cloth for her own household, with some over for the bigger family at Lordship Butlers.

Deliberately, Alys had chosen market-day for her visit. She was lucky: Uncle Richard and Aunt Joan, and young Joan, were all at the market and Adam was at school. Pentecost was alone: she had not much heart for the fun of village life since Avery died. She sat at the long table with her chin on her cupped hands — and Alys silently rejoiced.

'It's me Pentecost — Alys,' she said, as Pentecost hadn't responded to her shout. 'What are you doing?'

Pentecost rubbed her face with her fingers, and came back to reality. 'Thinking,' she said. 'Mother's talking about marriage for me already, Alys.'

'Oh dear,' said Alys. 'Won't Walter be upset!'

'I don't think I can bear to be married,' Pentecost went

on. 'So I have to settle in my mind — shall I become a nun?'

Alys was appalled. 'It's very holy and good, Pen,' she said. 'But how could you make up your mind to go away from here, for ever, and leave your family? You could never come back.'

'I'll go away anyway, when I marry,' said Pentecost with gloom. 'So will you, Alys. Though — ' she broke off awkwardly.

'If you were going to say I'm different, then I know I'm different,' said Alys. 'That's what I came to ask about. Please Pen, will you tell me? Please, Pen, do. I want to know who I am.'

Pentecost sighed sharply. 'You ought to be told,' she said. 'Jordan was on about it when he was here. He said it was a sin and a shame and the later they left it, the worse it would be for you.'

'I heard him,' said Alys. 'He said to my parents, "You should tell Alys." Somebody should.'

'Then I will,' said Pentecost. 'I'll be in dead trouble. But I'll tell you, Alys. You're not a Butler. You're a Castell.'

'But they're our enemies!' Alys burst out.

'There was a blood-feud,' said Pentecost. 'For years. Over a hundred years ago, Peter le Butler who was our ancestor fought to settle a quarrel with Reginald Castell. It was all proper and legal, and both men knew they might be killed.'

'How did they fight?' asked Alys. 'With broadswords?'

'I suppose so,' said Pentecost. 'Peter le Butler killed Reginald, and the Castells were so angry there was a hundred years of feud — Castell killing Butler, and Butler killing Castell, whenever they met.'

'Weren't they put in prison for it?' asked Alys.

'Once or twice, and they had to pay fines,' said Pentecost. 'But mostly they were too careful. People could never be caught, and things could never be proved.'

Alys was silent, thinking of the good horse, gone last year, and Avery a few weeks in his grave.

'Of course the Butlers blame the Castells, Alys,' said Pentecost. 'But Jordan always says we were as bad as them.'

'But what about me?' said Alys.

'Grandmother and grandfather wanted to stop it all,' said Pentecost. 'When grandfather came back from the war in France he was convinced that fighting was no use, and grandmother always said it was against the will of God. They met with the Castells and tried to arrange a peace. At the time when they met both families were going to have new grandchildren; and they agreed to exchange the babies, when they were born, and call them the Peace Children. Then when there was any risk of new fighting breaking out, each side was to look at its Peace Child and say — we can't hurt the family of this child, because we love it.'

'So I had a white dress,' said Alys. 'To show I was a Peace Child. Why didn't they tell me? I would have understood.'

'They thought you'd be upset,' said Pentecost. 'That you were too young.'

'Harry Brag isn't my father, is he?' Alys asked, struck by a new and horrible idea.

'No — he isn't old enough. Not much older than Avery was,' said Pentecost. 'Your father must be Harry's father, but I think you have a different mother. I can't tell you much, Alys; all I know is a few odd things Avery said.'

'Oh dear,' said Alys. 'It all seems so muddling. I half wish I didn't know; but I couldn't rest, not knowing. Is there any way I can prove who I am?'

'I suppose not,' said Pentecost. 'Though the Castells did send a token with you, when you were a baby. It was an icon: a little tablet of clay, with holy pictures stamped in it. Christ on the cross one side, and Our Lady with the Holy Child on the other. Sisely showed me once. It came from somewhere outside England.'

'I've seen it,' said Alys. 'Maud and I found it, looking inside mother's box. We never owned up that we'd seen inside the box; we knew mother had secrets in there. She usually locks it. I'm glad they sent something holy. Perhaps they aren't really so wicked — are they, Pen?'

'I don't know much more than you do,' said Pentecost. 'Avery used to swear they were Satan's own, especially Harry whom people call Harry Brag. But Jordan doesn't see it that way. Sir Philip, your father, never did us any harm. And your grandfather did try to make peace. Nobody was ever sure it was Harry and Robert who took Avery's horse, though Avery said so.'

'Do they live in a castle? They sound like it. They sound grand,' said Alys.

'There isn't a castle in East Hatley,' said Pentecost, and Alys sighed.

'So now you know,' said Pentecost after a silence. 'Will you tell them you know?'

'No,' said Alys and Pentecost nodded approval.

'Good,' she said. 'They love you, you know. As much as Maud or Rose. This thing makes no difference.'

'And I love them,' said Alys, thinking with a sudden surge of longing of the soft motherliness of Ede Butler and the happy rough-and-tumble of the Lordship Butlers life.

Alys went home slowly, the long way round, keeping her feet clean. 'It makes no difference,' said her thoughts. 'No difference . . .' But under her breath she muttered to herself, 'Alys Castell. Alys Castell. Alys Castell.'

It was not Alys's way to sit down, put her elbows on the table, and think out a problem. If it had been, she could never have sorted out what to do about her new knowledge: her mind was in too much of a turmoil — love for the Butlers, disturbance that they had not told the truth to her, and excitement at being somebody important, all coming one on top of another. She tried to keep calm, and to concentrate on what was going on at Lordship Butlers; but she kept trying to imagine the Castells and their surroundings, and feeling intense frustration because she couldn't do it. She might be sitting contentedly listening to the conversation of Hugh and Ede Butler, at the hearth, and would be suddenly distracted by wanting to picture her true father and mother, and having no idea at all what they were like. So many questions fretted her mind: had she got brothers and sisters (besides Harry and Robert) in East Hatley? And what was the house like there — the house that wasn't a castle? Was it grand and richly furnished, and did her mother wear gold rings? Would there be wild rejoicings, if she returned?

In the corners of her mind thoughts grew and decisions were reached without her actually planning them. A few days after her talk to Pentecost, she realized that she was not thinking 'if I returned', but 'when I return'. It was settled inside her that she would leave Lordship Butlers and try to find the Castells, and answer all these questions the only possible way; and that she would go in the autumn, in the last good travelling weather. She longed to talk to somebody about all this, but she didn't dare. Pentecost would feel bound to tell Ede and Hugh that 'their' Alys meant to leave them; Maud would burst into tears at the first word of such a thing; and joky, gossipy Emm would be a hopeless secret-keeper. With this particular secret, there was nobody she could trust.

She had the month of August, and part of September, to say goodbye to the farm. She walked or rode around with her face screwed up in an effort of attention, fixing in her memory the skyline — the ridge of hill with a crest of trees on it; the shape of the woodland around, the copses and spinney; the glorious flashing red of the poppies in the corn and the twinkling white and mauve of wild daisies and mallows by the road. She crossed and recrossed the little bridge over the moat — the moat which surrounded the buildings and farmyard of Lordship Butlers, and kept out — grandfather said — wild animals and wilder men. (Outside it she was still on the Butlers' land; but inside it she was home.) She sometimes hugged Ede Butler abruptly and for no obvious reason; Ede at times might scold, but she was a loving woman who liked small warm people clinging to her, and Alys usually had her hair stroked and sometimes a quick kiss — for Ede was always in a hurry. Nobody had time in that house to wonder why the children behaved as they did; and if they had, they would have expected upsets after the death of a dear cousin.

Harvest was a hectic time in Harlton, and this year a happy one: August was hot and dry and the carts came from the corn strips with good crops. Alys was there to clap and shout when the first sheaf was bound, and later when the last was carried in triumph round the field; and did her share of eating and singing at the harvest feast. And in the still-light evenings, there was a chance for dancing on the village green. Kit, the blacksmith's son, could sometimes be persuaded to get out his pipe and his little drum, and all the young people joined in round-dances or the winding follow-my-leader dance, the farandole, which the children loved. When he was home between journeys, Emm's eldest brother Sampson, who was a boatman, led the farandole. He was a lively fellow with a wicked look in his brown eyes, and he led them at first at a stately speed and then faster and faster — jumping the cow-pats which not all his followers successfully avoided, ducking under the low branches of trees, skidding over little ponds and ditches — while Kit ran to catch up with him, sometimes too breathless to play his pipe at all, and the little children at the back were half swung off their feet and tripped and stumbled and screeched, scarlet with laughter. Alys, in her goodbye mood of loving everybody, pulled even shy fat Maudlin from the big farm near the church into the snake of dancers, and gave her own hand ungrudgingly to cross-eyed Batt who suffered from warts.

Harvest-time, joyful as it was, couldn't last for ever; and one morning Alys woke to a smell of autumn — keen air with mist in it, ripe apples, and woodsmoke. A real end-of-September day, and she knew she was going.

She hadn't much to take. It all rolled into one bundle: her white dress and her blue overdress in the middle (to make a good impression) and wrapped around that a warm hood and a cloak, for the journey. The Castell icon she had taken from her mother's box, once careful watching had shown where Ede kept the key. She had made a little bag for this, out of a scrap of linen, and hung it round her neck on a string. She took her bundle out, with an old sack around it, and put it into a haystack while most of the family were breakfasting.

'Where are you going?' yawned Maud, still in bed, as Alys slipped out of the bedroom door.

'To do my egg-hunt,' said Alys.

'I thought it was my turn,' said Maud.

'I'm doing it, anyway,' said Alys. 'Are you complaining?'

'Not much,' said Maud, and went back to sleep.

Ursel was in charge of the poultry, but her early morning jobs included milking; so it was usually one of the girls of the family who combed the farmyard and stackyard for the brown or speckled eggs. 'Last time,' thought Alys, curling her hand around each delicate egg, smooth and often still warm. After she had carried the rush basket full of eggs in to the kitchen, she had her breakfast of runny porridge and skim milk, staring affectionately from one Butler to another Butler. Most of them got up quickly and rushed away from the table — Hugh Butler and Nicholas to see to the work of the farm, Ede and Sisely to the dairy to oversee Moll and Ursel there, grandfather to his second round of prayers, and Walter to organize some rabbit-hunting for after school. A fierce argument between him and Gilbert as to which pony was to be ridden by which boy, and whether the broken saddle could be used, echoed around the farmyard. Maud was down last, and was fighting for the last of the bread and cheese, the porridge being finished before she arrived.

To help the busy Ursel, Maud and Alys between them drove the geese over the bridge that crossed the moat and into the pasture. From there the village goose-herd would take them away to the strips of stubble where they could eat well on the fallen grain. It was goose-fattening time now; the victims for the Michaelmas feast were already fat, and people were beginning to think of Christmas time. The geese went in a noisy, straggling procession and the two girls chased them and hooshed them and laughed helplessly at their comic solemnity.

'You can manage a bit on your own now, can't you?' said Alys, as the flock settled down to graze. 'The goose-herd must be on his way.'

'Why, what are you going to do?' asked Maud.

'I'm off to Emm's for an hour, to play with her kittens,' said Alys. 'Don't tell mother!'

She ran back to the farm for her bundle, which she carried in her hotched-up skirt so that no one could see what it was. To everyone she met she called a different story. To Ursel, seen crossing the yard, it was 'Tell my mother I'm taking flowers up to the shrine on the hill'; to Walter, sitting outside mending an arrow, it was 'I'm going off to get hazel-nuts from the wood.'

'Oh good,' said Walter. 'Save some for me.'

'You get your own, Wat,' said Alys, and ran.

And to Sisely, scouring a wooden bowl at the house door, she called, 'I'm off with a loaf to Aunt Joan — she says she's not baking till Saturday.'

'Who's with the geese?' said Sisely.

'Maud,' called Alys, as she went.

That should keep them quiet for a time, she thought. By the time they've really missed me and they've looked at Emm's, and at the shrine, and at Aunt Joan's, and in all the hazel copses they can be bothered with, I should be safe at East Hatley, and with the Castells for ever.

On second thoughts, she didn't like the sound of 'for ever'.

'With the Castells,' she thought. 'At home.'

She shut her eyes to a sudden vision of Ede and all the Butler girls, singing as they spun, and thought of the new grand family and all the fuss they would be bound to make of their lost child — given up, but as by a miracle returned.

As she crossed the wooden bridge over the moat, Alys said a prayer for the home and the people she was leaving behind; and as she crossed the second bridge, over the stream which bounded the home meadow, and fed the moat waters, she said one for herself and her new life. That done, she skipped a few steps and swung her bundle and began to sing.

The green path which she followed across the fields was pleasant walking. Small farm carts used it, and riding-horses and people on foot; but heavier carts and carriages used the high road. At some times of the year the path would have been mud to the tops — or over the tops — of Alys's shoes; but now most of it was dusty dry and Alys walked easily between the ruts, where grass and plantains and mayweed made comfortable footing. Before long the path struck uphill and joined the ridge trackway, the Mare Way, which ran between trees.

Her great fear was of meeting people she knew, who would ask kindly where she was going and why she was on her own. No nice girl went about alone, and Alys was nervous of raised eyebrows and searching questions. In fact whenever, in the still morning air, she heard hoofbeats coming, she ducked behind trees and hid until the rider was past. This way she escaped the eyes of Uncle Richard, riding slowly and in a brown study with a great book balanced open on his saddle-bow (she guessed he had been to see the priest at Eversden, with whom he had long theological discussions and who often accused him of being a Lollard — no true believer). She also missed being seen by Dame Isabella Paunton, Maudlin's mother, riding with a man-servant behind her and looking important. Alys, while she lunched off a hunk of bread she had brought and some wayside blackberries, wove stories about where Dame Isabella had been. She guessed, discussing the marriage of one of Maudlin's elder sisters; there were four of them, the eldest already married, the others still to go.

The middle of the day grew hot, and Alys's feet grew tired of the rutted path, and her arms tired of her bundle. She started to calculate times and distances, but could only guess how far she had come. There were few landmarks to tell her where she was: she was in a quiet stretch of trackway, where the woods of Eversden and Arrington pressed close around the path, and the path was all shadows and damp slimy places. It was too quiet for her liking: she began to think of the wild boar which might come out of the thickets, and of all the ways in which the deep woods might be haunted. A phantom dog was said to run the woodland path (black, of course): Alys looked nervously at the bushes and listened for unusual rustlings. The sound of a horseman now would have been a comfort, but there was none to be heard.

What she did hear was the sudden noise of a walker coming up behind her. By the time she heard this traveller it was too late to hide: the traveller was catching up with her fast, and the track was straight. The footsteps suggested a long, assured stride. Alys looked back at once, and was relieved to see that the strider was a stooped (but still tall) old woman in a thick russet dress and a grey hood, carrying a covered basket.

'Wait for me, child — wait!' shouted the old woman; she need hardly have bothered, for at her speed she quickly reached Alys. Though Alys did think that the quick step faltered and the voice began to quaver just as the old woman caught up with her.

'Where are you bound for, little lady?' Alys was asked, as strikingly bold and bloodshot brown eyes peered at her under the grey hood.

'East Hatley, to my family,' said Alys. 'And you?'

'I'm going that way, too,' said the woman. 'With some bacon for my son. And what do you carry?'

'An old cloak that needs mending,' said Alys. She didn't like the way the old woman was eyeing her bundle and she didn't like the old woman's greyish, bristly chin.

'We'll go along together,' said her companion, holding out a friendly hand that was large, bony, and looked as though it could grip ferociously. Alys pretended not to notice it.

The woman, as they went, fired at Alys a whole string of questions about herself and her family. Alys gave wild and evasive answers, her suspicions more and more aroused by the questioner's nosiness and surprisingly gruff voice and how tall she seemed to be now that she was holding her shoulders straight. When they came down to a low boggy place where they had to walk in single file as the track narrowed, Alys hung back and fell in line behind her companion, and as the old woman lifted up her heavy skirt to keep it out of the mud Alys caught a glimpse of boots of good leather, with spurs.

Large boots, too: much more suitable in size as well as nature for a man than for a woman. Dreadful thoughts came into Alys's mind of the much-feared housebreaker nicknamed Long Lankin — a man who not only robbed but cut the throats of his victims. At once, she took a flying leap over the deep ruts at the edge of the pathway and ran blind at full pelt into the wood.

'Hoy!' shouted a loud and rough voice behind her, and with a noise like a charging bull the 'old woman' came crashing after her. But the sound of stamping feet suddenly finished with a tremendous thump. Alys didn't know whether her pursuer had caught his spurs in his skirt, or whether he had tripped over a root or a trailing branch: she made the best of her opportunity and ran for dear life.

She twisted and turned among the close-growing trees and bushes, keeping away from cleared areas and going as deep as she could into thickets. She must have run for half an hour, and when she stopped exhausted, the woods were silent around her. Hardly a bird sang, and there was no sound at all of feet or even lightly rustling branches. Alys lay flat in a cluster of hazel bushes and kept completely still until her own breath and pounding blood were quiet again and she could be sure there was nobody near. And after this she slept.

When she woke and stood up, brushed herself down, re-rolled her precious bundle and picked fragments of leaf and twig out of her hair, she admitted to herself at once she was hopelessly lost.

She had not come into the wood by any path, but paths there must be. Her only chance of getting out of the wood was to find a track of some kind and follow it. Otherwise she might wander in circles until she became too weak to go on any longer, and died where she fell.

'And while I'm looking, I'll look for water,' she told herself firmly. 'And nuts and berries.'

She started with a skimpy meal of hazel nuts, cracked between the heels of her two shoes, and followed it up with beechnuts and some very sharp crab-apples. Discovering a stream was an excitement: she drank, and followed its course, but it ended rather dismally in a swamp and a tiny pond with reeds in it. No sign of habitation and no sign of a path.

Alys began to be worried now about the failing light. She had no idea how long she had slept, but the sun was getting low and the thought of nightfall was alarming. Bitterly she wished she had taken a Butler horse for her journey. Perhaps it would have been stealing — but it would have been much safer than this long and weary drag on foot, and perhaps the Castells could have got the horse back somehow to the Butler farm.

She had wandered into an area where the trees were farther apart, and showed signs of recent coppicing. This at least looked more hopeful than the thickets and the swamp. She paused to scan the sky for signs of smoke, and the ground for signs of footprints: there was nothing. She also listened — for a barking dog, a cackling hen or goose — any noise of house or farm. She heard none of these, but she did hear the distant sound of horse-hooves growing steadily nearer. She thought at once of a man-woman, in skirt and spurs, mounted now to hunt down his quarry. There was no cover of shrubs and bushes at hand, so she slid behind the trunk of a sizeable ash tree — but the light grey of her dress must have shown her up. The rider drew level, stopped abruptly, and a voice shouted, 'Hi! Come out from there and be seen!'

Alys didn't. She didn't even look round the tree-trunk.

She heard the noise of the rider sliding to the ground, and turned to run; but before she had gone more than a couple of steps she was grasped by the shoulders and spun around. At least, she was relieved to see, it was not the 'old woman' in spurs who had caught her: it was a long and skinny, elderly man, true enough, but one whom she faintly recognized. He had been pointed out to her in the streets of Cantebridge, riding a destrier (a knight's war-horse) and wearing half-armour. Today he rode a serviceable cob and wore a long tunic of soft leather, and a rather jaunty little hat with a trim of fur all round it. She knew his reputation perfectly well: a landowner and one not afraid to flout the law when he felt like it. A bit of a brigand, although he was rich; a bit of a rebel, although he was powerful. Sir Baldwin St George, knight — and no better than he should be.

'Ah,' said Sir Baldwin. 'A little villein. Or is it? Nice fine wool for a dress, nice fine leather shoes under foot. More a lady than a villein, maybe. And if so — why on her own?'

Alys blushed, and brushed her hair from her face.

'I'm lost,' she said. 'Can you show me the way out of the wood, Sir Knight?'

'Better than that,' said Sir Baldwin. 'I'll take you. Come along.'

'You aren't lost yourself, then?' said Alys timidly.

Sir Baldwin laughed with a laugh like a donkey's neigh.

'What, in these woods?' he said. 'No fear. It's my hawk that's lost. I suppose you haven't seen a falcon?'

'No,' said Alys. 'Where's your austringer?' A knight of Sir Baldwin's age and eminence would have a hawk-master or austringer, to care for his birds.

'That's the devil of it,' said Sir Baldwin. 'The austringer's gone to look for the hawk, and only the holy angels know where they're at.'

He heaved Alys on to his cob, and swung himself up behind her. Alys tucked up her skirts, and sighed with relief.

'And where are you off to?' Sir Baldwin asked.

'East Hatley,' said Alys.

'Indeed,' said Sir Baldwin. 'That's useful. I'm going to Hungry Hatley myself, so I shan't be taken out of my way.' There was a curious inflection in his voice, as if he found her answer surprising. 'You'd best tell me your name too.'

Alys hesitated. 'Alys' she said at last, and hoped he would ask for no more.

'Yes, and the rest of it?' he insisted.

Alys knew well that Sir Baldwin, living in the next village to the Castells, would be aware that they had no daughter at home called Alys. She invented a plausible name for a fair-haired family: 'Alys White,' she said.

Sir Baldwin let out a short snorting laugh. 'Hang on then, Alys White,' he said, and put spurs to the horse. They bucketed off through the trees, Alys hanging on grimly to saddle and bundle. And when they were back on the rutted path between the hawthorns and the brambles, they still kept up a rapid trot interspersed with intervals of a jerky canter. Dark was really falling now, and Alys was heartily relieved that she was being swept towards East Hatley at a racketing good pace.

When the first cottages of the village appeared, and the pale-walled church showed up in the twilight, Sir Baldwin reined in his horse.

'East Hatley,' he said.

'Oh thank you, Sir Baldwin,' said Alys sincerely. She had been afraid he would carry her on to Hungry Hatley to serve as his kitchen-maid.

'A word or two before you thank me,' said Sir Baldwin, his arm still around her waist. 'I've eyes in my head, young woman, and I know well enough I've seen you before — and where.'

'In Cantebridge,' suggested Alys, hoping to turn his thoughts. 'At market.'

'Maybe, maybe not,' said Sir Baldwin. 'But I most certainly saw you in Harlton, at Bettris Paunton's wedding-feast. The one bright head among the dark ones, eh? Stood out a mile. White by colour — but Butler by name, I think, Mistress Alys?'

'And if I am?' asked Alys.

'And if you are — someone will be ready to pay a ransom for you without a doubt,' said Sir Baldwin. 'Now who will pay best, do you suppose? The Butlers, to have you rescued from the Castells? Or the Castells, to have you in their hands?'

'You're joking,' said Alys. 'Knights don't hold children to ransom. It's against the law.'

'No law holds me, child,' said Sir Baldwin. Alys thought that from all she had heard about him, this was certainly true.

'You're behind the times, Sir Baldwin,' she said. 'It's true that I was living with the Butlers: but only as a foster-child. The Castells are my kin and I have returned to them. Neither side would pay you anything for me, because I was fostered by agreement. Have you never heard of the Peace Child?'

'What!' said Sir Baldwin. 'Of course; an old story. Castell, are you? You have the look of them. They may give me thanks, then, for bringing you home, and as they're my tenants — as well as neighbours too near to quarrel in comfort — I've no wish in the world to fall out with them.'

'I didn't know the Castells didn't own the farm,' said Alys, her ideas about her family coming down a peg or two.

'Trying to buy it off me,' said Sir Baldwin. 'I'm not at all sure I shall sell. But I'll say this for them — their money's good. Go on, then — prove your story. Let's see you walk straight to their door.'

He lifted Alys off the horse and let her slide to the ground. She flexed her stiff hands and looked warily around her. In the thickening dusk she could not see any of the houses very well: but they all looked too small for the Castells' manor. Away beyond them, however, standing not far from the church and behind trees, she caught a glimpse of an imposing gatehouse, and behind it somewhere a flicker of light. The gatehouse dominated a bridge over a stream or moat: she could see the faint gleam of swans or ducks by the water.

'Thank you, Sir Baldwin,' she said with a curtsy. 'I shall tell my family you were kind.'

She made off, without a backward look, towards the gatehouse. Sir Baldwin said nothing, but let her go.

When she reached the bridge she found a gate on the village side of it: but it was not locked. She went with pretended confidence through, and curtsied again to Sir Baldwin as she turned to shut it behind her. He raised a hand, spurred his horse and was off at a good speed. Alys's guess must be right. She had come home.

It dismayed her a little that there was no light in the gatehouse. The bridge (of stone, this one) ended with a heavy wooden door filling an archway; the windows on either side showed no gleam of fire or candlelight.

Alys gave one or two thumps on the door, and then spotted a heavy bell on a bracket, with a knotted rope attached. She hauled on this and was rather alarmed at the clatter it produced — more a tinny rattle than a satisfying bong.

There was a quick result. A man's voice shouted something indistinguishable, and she heard the muffled rasp of the pulling of iron bolts. A little wicket in the main doors swung half-open and two suspicious faces, man and woman, peered out at her.

'Is this the Castells' manor?' said Alys, suddenly bereft of confidence.

'Yes, but they're not at home,' said the woman, holding the door. 'They're all at their other house. They're in London.'

'But I'm Alys Castell,' said Alys with as much command as she could. 'I've come to find my mother, and my father Sir Philip. Please let me in.'

'What?' said the man; and the woman, more aggressively, 'There's no Alys Castell. We know that.'

'Yes there is,' said Alys. 'Do you suppose you know all the Castell kin? I'm the Peace Child.'

'What?' said the man again.

'He's deaf,' said the woman briefly. 'We've to keep intruders out, and it's after curfew. You'd best come back in the morning.'

'I can't do that,' said Alys. 'Don't you understand? I've nowhere else to go, and I'm the Castells' child. I've come to find them — to live with them.'

'And I say they aren't here,' said the woman.

'Then who is here?' said Alys. 'Isn't there a steward, or a bailiff, in the house?'

'Lord, yes, there's Mistress Cheeseman and Master John,' said the woman. 'We only keep the gate. They'll be up in the house, and likely enough in their beds.'

'Then you must wake them up,' said Alys. She was undecided now between losing her temper, bursting into tears, or doing both. This was not her expected homecoming.

'Shoot the bolts, woman, and stop blethering,' said the deaf man. 'It's plain to see she must speak to Mistress Cheeseman. Follow me.'

He lit a candle in a horn lantern and set off at a good pace across the courtyard, hushing a few kennelled dogs as he went. Alys, unsure of her footing, hung on to the rough frieze of his sleeve. Even so she stumbled over bumpy cobbles and caught her foot on something which rolled away, bouncing — a wooden pail?

When they reached the house itself Alys was pleased to see a chink or two of light through the shuttered windows of the hall. The gatekeeper thumped the hall door, as Alys had thumped his gate, and shouted; and the door was opened almost at once by a neatly-dressed girl of about thirteen.

'Young lady,' said the gatekeeper. 'See Mistress Cheeseman.' And he turned and stumped off.

The girl took Alys through a door in a central passage, and into the hall itself. The fire at one end of it had been banked for the night, but still smoked warmly; and a few candles near it lit a small group of people drinking their nightcaps, which appeared to be portions of ale in dumpy mugs. A large, square-shouldered woman stood up to welcome Alys.

'You come late,' she said — politely, but it was a question.

'I've come to join my father and mother,' said Alys, 'but I'm told they aren't here. I'm Alys Castell.'

'You say father and mother, but we know nothing of you here,' said Mistress Cheeseman. 'Do you mean Sir Philip and Lady Annis?'

Alys was pleased to learn her mother's name. 'Yes,' she said. 'And you don't know me because I'm the exchanged one. I've been living with the Butlers. I'm the Peace Child.'

She expected delighted recognition at this, but she only met blank faces. The Castells did not appear to have taken their servants into their confidence when they exchanged a child.

The girl who had let her in, and who had been staring at her unblinking, spoke up.

'Whatever child she is, she's got the greatest look of the family that ever I saw,' she said. 'She's the dead spit of Mistress Jossey.'

'She is that,' said several voices.

'But how does it happen you arrive so late, Mistress, and all alone?' asked Mistress Cheeseman.

'Sir Baldwin St George brought me,' said Alys. 'He left me at the gate.'

The bearded man with a furred tunic who appeared to be the most important among them stood up. 'Find the child a bed, wife,' he said. 'And we'll all go to ours. This can be settled in the morning.'

Alys was given some rich and delicious soup and half-led, half-carried to the outbuilding where the woman servants slept, and rolled into a bed shared with the servant girl who had let her in.

'Tell me then,' the girl whispered to her in the dark. 'You're so sure of your welcome — whose child are you? Master's by some other woman, or madam's by some other man?'

Alys was scandalized. 'I'm the child of both of them,' she said.

'How come then you were farmed out to another family so long?' said the girl. 'There's things you haven't been told yet, I'll dare swear.'

'Some things, but not that. I'm the Peace Child,' said Alys. The girl only giggled.

'What are my sisters' names?' said Alys, and listened hungrily as she was told. She went to sleep thinking over and over, 'Christina — Annora — Jossey.' But remembering, all the same, Sisely, Julian, Maud, Rose — and Ede Butler, whom she must learn not to call mother even in her thoughts.

Alys woke in the first sunlight, in an empty bed. She felt around for Maud or Rose, realized they weren't there, and sat up in the shock of lostness. The half-shuttered window was in the wrong place, the roof was too low, there was no bed in the corner for Julian and Sisely. She remembered she was in East Hatley, and felt cold and small with loss and longing. If someone would set her on the right road, she could be back in Harlton by dinner-time, with a story of wandering in the wood, pursued by Long Lankin. She got up hurriedly, and went down into the court to find the women's privy. A strange maidservant directed her and waited for her, to show her where the water was for washing and to lead her in to the hall where smoke already rose from the open hearth and half a tableful of people sat at breakfast. Master Cheeseman got up and led her to an empty seat, bowing politely.

Alys drew her breath to tell him she was going back to Harlton, but he was already speaking.

'Plans have been made for your conveyance to London, Mistress Alys,' he said. 'It's not all we could wish: there is no good carriage to be had in Hatley — my lady's has gone up to London with her; our farm carts are in the fields; and there's nobody we can spare to ride with you. But Jack Carter and his wife Sib are making the journey to Ware today; they'll take you that far, and they'll be given money to pay for your carriage on, tomorrow, with some safe party. It won't be handsome travelling, but I've seen to it that there's clean straw in the cart. Will you be satisfied to travel this way?'

'What else will be in the cart?' said Alys, thinking of pigs.

'Flour-bags and apples,' said Mistress Cheeseman. 'Are you satisfied?'

'Yes, and thank you for your trouble,' said Alys politely. Harlton slipped away as if it were a bird going into clouds or a trout into the weeds of the stream: it was too late for that.

Alys's breakfast had to be hurried, because Jack Carter was waiting. She had porridge, and milk; and Mistress Cheeseman packed her a little basket of bread and meat and a couple of melting golden pears. Master Cheeseman gave her a piece of parchment with her parents' London address on it in spiky letters. After that Alys, wrapped in her cloak for warmth, was hoisted into the cart which stood outside the gate, beyond the bridge; Jack Carter glared sourly and seemed to think the whole venture an ill-timed nuisance and Sib was no more friendly. Jack had two horses, harnessed head-to-tail, for his light cart, and Alys felt reasonably confident of the safety, even if not the cheerfulness, of her transport.

She settled herself on a layer of straw, called goodbye to the Cheesemans and the gate-keepers, and tried to accustom herself to the bumping and lurching as the cart set off. The horses were wide awake and lively, and East Hatley church roof and smoking house-tops soon disappeared as the road went into trees. Alys watched for a time, enjoying the colour of browning leaf-shocks and the changing cloud of the sky; but soon she pulled a flour-bag behind her head and drifted off to sleep. Sib Carter sat up in the front of the cart by Jack, ignoring Alys.

Rain woke her: not heavy, but a cold drizzle which damped her face and hands and clung to the rough material of her hood and cloak. The brightness of the day was all gone, and Alys was miserable to think of travelling many more miles in the open cart. She walked up its rocking length and tapped Sib on the back.

'Where are we?' she asked. 'Is it still a long way to Ware?'

It was Jack who answered. 'Matter of sixteen miles,' he said, not turning his head.

'Can't you make the horses go any faster?' said Alys. 'I'm getting wet.'

'Find yourself a sack. Plenty on the floor there,' said Jack Carter. He made no effort to speed the horses up. Alys covered her head and shoulders with empty sacks, and made the best of it.

A few miles further on, with the rain falling more heavily, Jack Carter suddenly pulled up his horses. Alys pushed aside her top sack and looked around. She saw only a desolate stretch of country, the road bordered by woodland, and no habitation in sight.

'This is where you get down,' said Jack Carter over his shoulder.

'What do you mean?' said Alys. 'Is there a tavern here?'

'Not for miles,' said Jack, opening his mouth in a silent laugh showing a few dark yellow teeth.

'What, then?' said Alys.

'Get out,' said Sib. 'This is as far as we're taking you.'

'But you're taking me to Ware,' said Alys. 'And paying my carriage on.'

'Oh, are we?' said Jack, and laughed again. 'What Jack gets, Jack keeps.' He patted the leather pouch at his belt. 'And now get down, or I'll come and throw you down.'

'You'll be sent to prison, or hanged,' said Alys desperately. 'I'm Alys Castell.'

'Oh? And who's she? Somebody's little mistake, from what I hear,' said Sib. And Jack suddenly bellowed 'Get down!' with such force that the horses shifted uneasily and the cart pitched. Seeing no help for it, Alys threw down her little roll of clothes, and her basket, and climbed down after them. Sib gave her a push to help her on her way.

'Give me some money, at least, Jack Carter,' Alys begged, standing in the road. 'Or I may starve.'

'Your kind don't starve,' said Jack. 'My kind starve — unless we take what we can get.' He slapped up his horses and the cart rumbled away, Sib looking back with a triumphant grin. Alys stood alone in the road.

She had no idea of where she was in terms of distance from East Hatley, or Harlton, or Ware; no idea whether to go on towards Ware, or try to make her way back to Hatley. As she stood bedraggled, getting wetter every minute, she heard a horse coming up from the way she had come: and stood still, expectant, thinking of Sir Baldwin and hoping for a lift.

The horse was fully loaded, though: a thickset man in front and a very stout lady behind, and panniers bulging between them. Alys called out to them all the same.

'Please,' she shouted. 'How many miles to Ware?'

'Twelve, about,' said the man, reining in his horse and staring openly at Alys. 'Are you travelling alone?'

'I wasn't, but I've been abandoned,' said Alys. 'Where's the nearest house, where I can stop?'

'Ahead, on the bridge,' said the woman, and laughed like one amused. 'Walk on — it isn't far. She'll take you in.' They rode on, both chuckling, and left Alys wondering about 'she'.

To two fat people on a trotting horse it might not seem far, but to Alys trudging through the rain it was a good two miles before she saw the bridge. She passed several people going the opposite way from her, and several carts overtook her at a good pace; but she held on for the house ahead.

The bridge, when it appeared, was not spanning a river, but a deep, quick-flowing stream; and it was a hump-backed affair with room for a broad waggon just to squeeze across. Beside it was a tiny round hut, with slit windows and a thatched roof. Alys gave a silent prayer of thanks and almost ran towards it.

She had hoped for a welcome, but she had not expected one quite so emphatic. While she was still several paces from the hut a figure shot out, seized her, and dragged her inside at a run. Alys saw through the blur of the rain a gaunt, grinning face, a draggle of hair as tangled as waterweed, arms whirling in the long loose sleeves of a tattered gown. She was so terrified she even tried to struggle free and run for it — but run where?

The inside of the hut was dim with smoke and lit only by its thin window-slits and gaps in the shaggy thatch. But Alys could see that the creature holding her was a woman, and quite a young one. Under the dirt and grease there might have been a pretty face, and bright hair: but the expression was one of greed and malice, and Alys was still afraid.

'Spare a penny, young madam, for the poor hermit,' said the woman. 'A penny — or two.'

'Oh, are you a hermit?' said Alys. She had seen people

before who lived solitary in chapels on bridges and asked for charity from travellers. 'Is the money for the poor?' she asked.

'For the poorest of all,' said the woman. 'Who's so poor as God's beggars? For the money you shall have my prayers to see you on your journey safe. Come on, now! Money for the poor hermit.'

'I haven't any,' said Alys. 'I never had. I know you'll say people don't travel without money: but Jack Carter drove off with my fare and left me stranded.'

'That Jack!' said the hermit. 'I know him. But you must have money. I can't let you go unless you give me money.'

'Not let me go!' said Alys. 'What good will that do?'

'A little maid hermit to wait on me, and help me,' said the woman. 'A pretty little maid hermit to tempt the travellers in and say the prayers. I'm sure you pray well. Yes, and you can learn my skills from me. I can cure the sick,' (she was whispering close to Alys's ear). 'With a potion of bats' heads, or an oil of spiders — '

'Shush!' said Alys. 'That's sorcery. You could be burned. I won't learn sorcery.'

'That's as may be,' said the hermit. 'But if you won't learn, mistress, I can still keep you here to work and pray and keep the fire in. So that I can sleep.'

Alys was silent. She was fairly sure now that the hermit was mad.

'Or give me money,' said the hermit. She opened Alys's cloak to see if there was a purse hung on Alys's belt. Alys tugged free, offended by the hermit's prying fingers and her strong smell.

'I've got some bread and meat and two pears — we can share it,' she said, remembering the basket. There wasn't much sharing. The hermit wolfed the meat and most of the bread, and guzzled the pears so that syrup dripped from her chin. Alys only got a corner of the loaf.

The hermit washed down her meal with huge swallows from an earthenware jug. After this she rolled herself in a blanket by the fire and fell into a snoring sleep. Alys crept around the hut to test how deep the sleep really was. She took a drink of sour milk from a different jug (the one the hermit had emptied smelt of beer), put a log on the fire from a pile in a dry corner, and sat by the smoky warmth for a time to dry her feet. Then, judging that the hermit was very sound asleep indeed, she tucked her bundle into Mistress Cheeseman's basket, tiptoed to the door, and ran for the bridge as hard as she could go. There was no noise behind her.

The rain had stopped, and though the puddles in the road soon soaked her feet Alys went on more cheerfully, with a sense of having escaped from peril. 'Better the open road than shut in a hut with a hermit,' she said to herself. 'If that isn't a proverb, it ought to be.'

All the same, she was anxious. It must now be well into the afternoon: the sun was westering. With no money, and little trust left in the friendliness of strangers, where should she spend the night?

She didn't know whether to be more hopeful, or more fearful, when she heard the hoof-falls of several horses from behind.

Alys's first thought was to hide. She guessed, though, that the riders had already seen her: the road was flat and hedgeless here, the few trees had had their lower branches eaten away by browsing animals and there was no overhang. She stood her ground and looked back at the oncoming travellers, and at once was overcome with relief.

For surely they were pilgrims. There was a group of riders — about eight — and behind them lurched along a gaudily painted cart with a canvas cover stretched over arched supports. Alys had often seen small bands of pilgrims, travelling east to Walsingham or back from there to London; these perhaps were homeward bound. Many of them broke their journey in Haslingfield, close by Harlton, and worshipped at the shrine on the hill. Pilgrims could be appealed to; pilgrims were safe. Mellow with religious satisfaction — vows fulfilled, candles lit, prayers said — they would be only too ready, she calculated, to do an act of charity.

The riders were still some way off when Alys shouted to them.

'Holy pilgrims!' she called to the first ones, 'will you help a fellow-traveller? My fare has been stolen from me and I'm all alone.'

'Gog's bones!' said the first rider, and burst into a roll of giggles. 'Save you, child, but we aren't pilgrims. We're the devil's children, us, and the devil's the one who'll get us.'

Alys stared at him, uncertain. He was a pleasant-looking young man, neat and clean, the long tail of his hood wound round and round his neck and a belt studded with bright chunky stones circling his waist.

'What are you then?' she said.

'Musicians, at your service,' said a second man. His horse did not like being stopped on the road and fidgeted, throwing up its head.

'A travelling band of musicians, going to Westminster to make our fortunes,' said the first man. 'My name is Hawkyn Harper, and my neighbour here is Roger Hall. And who are you, and what's your history?'

Alys told him as quickly as she could, while Roger's horse continued to give trouble and the rest of the troop caught up with them.

'So I have to get to London, to Sir Philip Castell,' Alys concluded. 'His address is written here: I'll show you.' She fetched the scrap of parchment from her sleeve.

'Castell,' said Hawkyn, and he exchanged a glance with Roger.

'Heard of him,' said Roger. 'Shipowner, isn't he? With a son at court.'

Hawkyn whispered something, of which Alys only caught two words, 'rich' and 'influence'. She judged things were going well for her.

'We'll take you to your father, Mistress Alys,' said Roger finally. 'If you don't mind simple transport. Will you come up behind me, or will you ride in the cart?'

'The cart, thank you,' said Alys. 'It's going to rain again.'

The cart, she realized as Hawkyn led her to it, already had occupants. Two female heads, with elaborate head-dresses of beads and netting, were peering out at the side under the lifted canvas, laughing at a shared joke.

'Who's this, then, fellows?' shouted one of them to Roger.

'Mistress Alys Castell,' said Roger, raising his eyebrows. 'Make her welcome. These two ladies, Alys, are Tillot and Ibb.'

'Ladies!' shrieked Ibb, and the two girls shook with what seemed to be uncontrollable laughter.

But they were kind enough. They pulled off Alys's wet shoes, and spread her cloak to dry; and they gave her a pasty and a mug of ale. Alys listened for a while to their conversation, about clothes and hairstyles and a certain Mistress Joan they didn't think very well of. Some men's names were mentioned, and their voices sank to whispers. Alys studied the trunks and boxes in the cart, and such musical instruments as were visible — Hawkyn's harp, a large drum, a pair of bagpipes. She guessed that the smaller ones were in boxes, packed in sheepskins and hay. The whole floor of the waggon was covered with hay; there were even spare sheepskins in a heap. Alys rolled herself up in these, and lay warm and as comfortable as the jolts of her transport would allow, listening to the pattering of rain on the canvas overhead. She slept.

What woke her was the bumping of the cart over cobbles, a huge clatter of horse-hooves, dogs barking and a squawk of hens. They were arriving somewhere.

'Is this Ware?' she asked, brushing hair out of her eyes as she sat up.

'Lord, no,' said Ibb, who was peeping out under the canvas, letting chill air through the gap. 'You've no sense of the country, Alys Castell. We shan't make Ware till tomorrow.'

'Royston?' said Alys, thinking backwards.

'You slept through Royston,' said Tillot. 'We're near Barkway now.'

'Is it a tavern?' Alys asked.

'We can do better than taverns,' said Ibb. 'We're minstrels. This is a grand house and we shall have all the best — fire and food and cosy beds.'

Alys revised her ideas. Minstrels had sometimes visited Lordship Butlers and played and sung during or after dinner; they had always been given the best the house could provide. It was clearly a case, though, of 'sing for your supper', and what could she do for hers? She smoothed down her hair and thought.

The house was certainly grand, and the welcome was warm. A crowd of eager servants came running out to hold the horses and lead them to trough and stable; the instruments were unloaded with care and Alys was lifted out of the cart by a stout young man with a greasy face. She would rather have jumped.

'Is that all you've got to wear?' asked Ibb as the three girls tidied themselves in the long bedroom where all the women servants slept. Ibb herself had got out a scarlet dress with trimmings of gold cord, and Tillot was already changing into a green one with fur on it. 'You do look a bit of a country girl, if I may say so.'

Alys recollected her bundle, and to the approval of the other two she put on her white 'peace' dress with her blue overdress above it.

'*That's* more like it,' said Ibb. 'Now then — let's find a crown for you. 'Tillot combed out Alys's tangly hair and Ibb put a fillet of gold braid and shining stones on her head. 'Now you look more like a little minstrel girl,' she said. 'Hold your head up and think you're tall. You'll do us credit.'

Alys went behind the other two girls into the great hall and curtseyed to the company, already sitting down for their meal. The men, especially, cheered and shouted. Alys felt extremely shy but would have had to admit she was enjoying herself.

She didn't need to be told that the custom for minstrels was 'Play first, eat afterwards' — even if it meant that you usually got your food cold. As the party of musicians went across the hall to find the staircase going up to the minstrels' gallery, her mouth watered at the sight and smell of fish in egg sauce, chicken in almond milk, spicy lamb stew, and sugared peaches. She had not had a good meal for two days.

While eating and conversation went on in the hall below, Hawkyn and Roger and the others got out their instruments and sang and played to entertain the party — especially those sitting at the high table, the opposite end of the room. Alys stood with them and tapped a little drum, careful to remain unobtrusive. She was surprised at how good the music sounded; they were better than any troop she had heard in Harlton, lively and rhythmic. Perhaps they would really make their fortunes in Westminster. Ibb and Tillot joined in some of the singing, with bright, high voices.

'What does the little girl do?' asked a boy of about Alys's age, sitting underneath the gallery. 'Can she dance on her hands?'

His remark came just after the end of a song and most of the hall heard it. One of the adults near the gallery shouted up, 'What about the child, masters? Does she dance and do tricks?'

Alys stood forward and curtsied. 'My mother wouldn't like me to dance in front of an audience,' she said. 'But I can sing.'

Roger gave her a sharp look, but the important people at the high table called out, 'Let her sing! Let's hear her,' so Alys knew she was to do her share to earn her good food.

All the Butlers sang, and Alys knew the songs that went with the favourite games and the country songs which marked the farmers' year — May carols, sheep-shearing and haymaking and harvest songs, and the popular songs and ballads sung at fairs as well. She picked a song about a girl who lived out in the fields, eating wild flowers and drinking spring-water, 'Maiden in the moor lay', and sang her loudest and her best. Hawkyn knew it too, and accompanied her softly on the harp. It was a question-and-answer song, and the listeners soon picked up the idea and the tune and sang the alternate lines back to Alys. After the first few bars Roger visibly relaxed; Alys would not disgrace him.

She was encored, and her second song was a spring song, about budding twigs and a young girl's scorn for the lover who had promised her his heart and then changed his mind. It had a chorus which Ibb and Tillot joined in, gently humming:

'Now springs the spray.
All for love I am so sick
That sleep I never may.'

The audience banged the tables heartily at the end of it, and Alys knew she was a success and had paid her way.

When the company had all finished and gone, the minstrels had their dinner at a side-table, together with the pages who had waited at the high table earlier. These were mainly boys between nine and thirteen: five of them, one as blond as Alys herself and with a very snooty air. Alys stared at them but they only talked to each other. They were not interested in minstrels, and certainly not in little girls.

She slept soundly that night, full of food and praise, between Ibb and Tillot in a feather bed.

The next day seemed dull by comparison. The weather was better and the three girls rode pillion most of the day, changing from one horse to another at intervals to give the horses a chance to recover from a double load. In spite of Ibb's scornful words about taverns, they dined in an inn at Ware. They paid for their food, Alys noticed, but the drink was free — in exchange for some noisy music, with a lot of drum to drown the babel of the drinkers and to attract new ones in. They got beds for the night at Waltham Abbey; no feather mattresses here, but a row of straw palliasses on the ground. 'Beggars can't be choosers,' said Tillot. 'We'll sleep better tomorrow night — eh, Ibb?' They giggled and Alys asked no questions. She thought, a little fearfully, that tomorrow she would be sleeping in her father's house.

And so they came into London, on a heavy grey morning which damped their spirits a bit. The nearer they got to the great city, the more traffic they met: the riders could dodge between other riders, but the lumbering cart was hard to manoeuvre and slowed their progress badly.

Alys fretted: she was anxious now to get to the Castells' well before curfew — at best, in time for dinner.

They went into the city by a stone-arched gate. There were severed heads of criminals, brown and rotting, stuck up on poles on the walls beside the gate as a warning to others, and crows flapped around them. After one horrified look Alys turned her eyes down, feeling sick.

Once they were well inside the walls their speed of travel was even slower. The cart now had to be led, as the law laid down, by a man walking at the head of the leading horse. It was just as well, because the streets were narrow and very crowded, and the camber, and the deep gutters down their middles, were a peril to the cart. The long poles carrying greenery, which stood out as signs from the ale-houses, were sometimes so low that they menaced the canvas top of the cart (and even the riders' hats); and around the horses' feet was a complication of dogs, children, and even escaped geese and pigs. Men and women with goods to sell shouted out from their shops, which were often little sheds attached to the fronts of the houses; and beggars — some with scabby faces, some with deformed or shrivelled limbs — put out clutching hands towards the passers-by. In some streets, there were some horrible smells.

Alys thought she had never seen so many people — that she wouldn't have believed there were so many people in England, let alone all together in one town. Part of her enjoyed the racket and looked with pleasure at shops and stalls, and the furred caps and mantles of the elegant rich; but another part of her would have confessed to panic and headache.

She was a little embarrassed, too, by the knowledge that the minstrels were making a detour to find Swan Lane and her father's house. Their business was in Westminster where, Roger told her as they rode, they hoped to be allowed to perform at the king's palace — or at least to some of the noblemen of his court.

'Doesn't the king have his own musicians?' asked Alys.

'That's the joy of it,' said Roger. 'He does, and no one else can normally get a look in. But his chief fiddler is a Fleming, and he's away in Flanders now because his father's ill. So the story goes. We thought we might have a chance.'

'So you should,' said Alys. 'You deserve it.'

It was mid afternoon when they got to Swan Lane, the sky now dark with threatening violet clouds. Alys was deeply thankful when the whole cavalcade halted outside a handsome gatehouse, with a sign showing a stately ship hung above it; and Roger Hall hammered on the door and asked to speak with Sir Philip Castell.

It surprised Alys that this town house, Ship House, was so like a country one. The River Thames was running at the bottom of the street, but couldn't be seen from the house, though the shouting from the landing-stage on the bank, and the squawks of seagulls, could be heard. The house did have some brick in its construction, unlike the houses at Harlton. It also had, like any manor, its internal courtyard; but this one was a garden, the hens and the few pigs enclosed and the rest of the space (apart from a turning place for carts) planted with herbs and southernwood and roses. There was no defensive tower, and no moat, but the door which led into the passage between hall and kitchen was just like the one at Lordship Butlers.

A servant admitted Roger Hall and led him away to talk to Sir Philip; Alys was left standing in the great hall. This had a feature new to Alys and which seemed to her the last word in sophistication: an inside staircase leading up to a wide gallery off which upstairs rooms opened. At the top of this staircase, looking down, was a girl. A glass-filled window shed some light on her face and her pale hair: it could have been Alys's own face, reflected in a hidden mirror.

'Who are you?' said the upstairs girl, and her manner was distinctly haughty.

'Your sister,' said Alys.

'You're not my sister,' said the other girl, staring down.

'I've got three sisters,' said Alys. 'Christina, and Annora, and Jossey. You're' — and she guessed — 'Jossey.'

'You're not my sister,' the upstairs girl reiterated. 'You're a villein.'

'I'm not a villein,' Alys flashed back. 'Sir Baldwin St George knew I wasn't a villein. I'm dressed for travelling, that's all.'

'You may have fooled Sir Baldwin —' began the upstairs girl; but she was interrupted by the hurried, fussy entry, through a door near Alys, of a stout, middle-aged man accompanied by Roger Hall.

'Is this the child?' he said, bustling up to Alys. 'And she told you she was mine?'

'She isn't,' shouted down the girl above.

Roger Hall looked up at her, and down at Alys, and began to laugh. 'She told me she was yours, Sir Philip, and if I believed her before I believe her doubly now,' he said. 'Between one sister and the other, what's in it but a couple of inches! As like as two peas in a pod.'

Sir Philip stared keenly at Alys, and Alys curtsied to her father.

'I am the Peace Child, sir,' she said. 'Alys Castell, and I have come home.'

'You said you could prove it,' Roger reminded her.

'So I can,' said Alys. She pulled out of the front of her dress the icon in its linen bag, and put it into her father's hand. Sir Philip slid it out of the bag and gave a shout of recognition.

'It is — it's my child!' he said; and grabbing Alys's hand he ran headlong up the stairs, dragging her after him. At the top he pushed open a door and erupted into a room where a long window, glazed, lit a woman and two girls who sat sewing, and a small boy playing fivestones at the woman's feet. Alys stopped dead, pulling free of her father's hand, her whole being concentrated on the woman — for this was her mother.

Sir Philip tugged her forward with an arm round her shoulders. 'My dear wife,' he said to the woman, 'see here . . . look!' He seemed to have run out of words.

Alys knelt down at her mother's feet and kissed the long pale hand which had dropped thread and needle, and felt cold to her lips. Her mother sat like a statue, staring at her.

'Madam,' said Alys, mindful of her manners, 'I am Alys. I've come back.'

'Did they send you?' whispered Annis Castell. 'Are they tired of you?'

'No, they love me,' said Alys. 'They don't know I've come.'

'Is there a letter?' Annis said, still whispering. 'Is there proof?' She seemed only half to understand what Alys had said.

'She had this,' said Sir Philip, and he put the icon into his wife's hand.

Alys's mother clutched it, kissed it, dropped it, and clasped her hands at her chest, fighting for breath. From white she turned to red, and broke into a mixture of convulsive sobbing and laughter. Alys was terrified. She was getting the most disconcerting welcome.

The two elder girls brought their mother water and put wet cloths to her forehead and neck; this seemed to calm her, and soon she drank some water and pulled Alys to her side.

'You've run away!' she said. 'They were cruel to you!'

'No,' said Alys patiently. 'They loved me. But you are my real mother, and I chose to come to you.'

'Chose!' said Sir Philip. 'Hear that — chose! There speaks a Castell. How old are you, Peace Child? Ten?'

'Nine,' said Alys; and her mother added, 'Ten in November.'

'And you did this all on your own?' said Sir Philip. 'Amazing!' He seemed to be puffed with pride.

'I had adventures,' said Alys. 'Until Master Hall and Master Harper took me in charge.'

'Master Hall — he's waiting,' said Sir Philip. 'I must do something for him.'

'He spent money on my account, sir, because I was robbed,' said Alys. 'A dinner and a lodging.'

'I shall do something for his company,' said Sir Philip, importantly.

'He wants to perform with them at Westminster. They're very good,' Alys called as her father trotted away. She would have run to the head of the stairs and called a goodbye, and thanks, to Roger; but her mother clung to her.

Her father had business and had to stay in his counting-house, but Alys spent the rest of the afternoon telling and retelling the story of her journey to an absorbed audience. Christina took up her sewing again while she listened, smiling slightly and now and then looking up to smile direct at Alys; the others sat with idle hands and threw in comments and questions. The hermit fascinated them most. Even Jossey stayed on her stool near Alys, intent.

Over dinner, which they ate downstairs in the hall with all the members of the household, Alys retold her story for her father's benefit. He laughed a good deal, and drank a good deal, and evidently regarded Alys's arrival as a matter to celebrate. She was glad of that.

After dinner the family returned upstairs, to their drawing-room (they called it the solar). A fire had been lit and it was a bright and cheerful room. The floor was covered with hay and the walls with tapestries, rich with red and blue thread; Alys thought it extremely elegant and far above any room at Lordship Butlers.

'Tell about the Butlers,' said Edward, leaning on Alys's

knee. 'Are they dreadfully wicked? They must be: they're the Black Butlers.'

Alys was shocked. Edward was only five — much too young to have such ideas. Who had been talking to him — Harry Brag?

'They're called the Black Butlers because they nearly all have black hair,' she said. 'And thick black eyebrows. Except my mother —'

Jossey pounced. 'Your foster-mother,' she said.

Alys blushed. 'My foster-mother,' she agreed. 'But they are the nicest, kindest people, and most loving to me.'

'What, even that wild fighting-man, Sir Steven — one of the heroes of Poitiers?' asked Sir Philip, raising thin blond eyebrows. 'A famous swordsman, and a fine man in a charge, but a dirty fighter by all accounts.'

Alys thought of the stooped old man with the lame leg, and his patient counselling of peace.

'Not now,' she said. 'He says war is waste, and the king should tell my Lord of Buckingham to bring his army home from France.'

'Does he indeed!' said Sir Philip, eyebrows up again.

'He made a pet of me,' said Alys. 'He called me Lily-flower.'

Her father suddenly smiled.

'I shall tell you all about them, Edward,' said Alys, 'tomorrow when there's lots of time. All their names, and what they do. Just think — I had three foster-brothers, and three boy cousins. Until Avery died.'

Sir Philip abruptly changed the conversation, and Alys, silent for almost the first time since she had arrived, observed her family.

Her father was not very tall, and his hair — thinning on the forehead — was bright gold. Her mother was as tall as he, and pale, and her hair was so light it was almost silver. Christina, fifteen years old, had her father's golden hair and was slender but not tall; Annora and Jossey, thirteen and eleven, were nearly as flaxen as their mother and both tall and bony: all the girls had Annis's rather sharp features. Edward was silver-haired, skinny and — Alys thought — decidedly spoilt. But one thing bothered Alys as she took stock of her family. It was not complete.

When Edward was dismissed to bed, fetched by his nurse, Alys changed her seat and sat down next to Jossey. Jossey was sewing, a candle at her elbow, and paid no attention to Alys; but Alys was not put off.

'Where's the other one?' she whispered.

Jossey didn't look up from her sewing. 'My older brothers, do you mean?' she said. 'Or half-brothers I should say — my father has been twice married, and they are the sons of his first wife. Harry and Robert: Harry is in Westminster, serving the king; Robert is a scholar, at the Inner Temple: he is going to follow the law.'

'I didn't mean them,' said Alys. 'There must be another child. A boy, I think.' She would have found it hard to explain to this unfriendly new sister that she wanted the other Peace Child: she wanted to see a dark head, with black Butler eyebrows, among all these strangers, and a warm-hearted Butler grin.

'Oh, Humfrey,' said Jossey. 'Humfrey is at our uncle's in Essex. He is a page there, learning good manners and court ways. He'll learn fighting too.'

'Is he younger than you?' said Alys. The Peace Child must be her own age.

'A little bit,' said Jossey, and inexplicably laughed.

'And what's he like?' asked Alys.

'You'll see him,' said Jossey, suddenly impatient. 'Our uncle will come to Westminster before Christmas, and Humfrey will come to pay his respects to his parents. You can wait till then.'

'Alys!' said her father's voice, suddenly stern. 'Whispering in corners is not polite. If you have anything to say, speak to the company.'

Alys apologized, feeling tears prickle behind her eyes.

She had a sense that being a Castell might be a good deal more strenuous than being a Butler.

'Alys should go to bed,' said her mother. 'Annora, Jossey, one of you will have to move. One of you can share with Christina and Alys can have half your present bed.'

Neither Annora nor Jossey looked best pleased, and Alys felt this was a bad beginning.

'I thought, madam, Alys might come into my bed,' said Christina. 'For the smallest to sleep with the largest would be a convenient arrangement.'

'Settle it how you please,' said Annis; and Alys was grateful for Christina's diplomacy.

As she curtsied goodnight to her father, Alys said, 'Sir, will you write to the Butlers? To say I'm here?'

'I have written,' said Sir Philip. 'I've said you came of your own free will — that it was your own thought; and that you are safe arrived and will stay with us. For good.'

For good, Alys wondered, or for not-so-good? But it was too late for wondering now: she had burned her boats.

Over the next few weeks, Alys's struggle to become a Castell was intense. At times she wondered if she would ever succeed; or whether she would always be obviously the odd one out. A lily among lilies, now, she didn't have to be self-conscious about her looks; but her behaviour, and her whole cast of thought, seemed to be vastly different from her family's.

The Castells were quiet people, rather stiff in their speech and manner; the girls, especially, had been trained to be silent and reserved (though Alys could not help being aware that Harry and Robert were not the only two in the family with quick tempers — besides herself, of course). Alys thought them cold and, sometimes, dull; they thought Alys's free and easy ways unbelievably lax, and Jossey — the most often heard — frequently called her a villein.

'You mustn't say "mother" and "father" when you talk about them,' she told Alys for the sixth or seventh time on a wet Saturday afternoon. 'You say "our honoured parents" or "our worshipful father" or whatever it is. Didn't the Butlers teach you anything?'

'They taught me love,' said Alys, suddenly angry. 'Not fine talking, and nothing inside it but puff.'

'I thought you liked puff,' said Christina, gently teasing; and Alys forgot her bad temper in a laugh. Puff was a delicious light, soft bread which she had never had at Lordship Butlers, and made the most of in Ship House.

'They didn't teach you to read,' said Annora, touching on a sore point.

'There was never time,' said Alys. 'I'd like to learn now, though. And to write. Can you write?'

'Ladies don't need to write,' said Jossey. 'We can all

read, and one of my honoured father's clerks can write for us if we need it.'

'I should like to learn to write,' said Alys. 'And to do figures too. Then I could help my father.'

Her sisters laughed, and Annora said, 'Bless you, Alys, Sir Philip has eight or nine clerks in his counting-house. He doesn't need you.'

Alys said nothing, and looked down. For a moment she had forgotten herself: she had been thinking of Hugh Butler, frowning over his bailiff's long accounts — the checking of which took up too much of the good daylight when he would have liked to be in the fields with a hawk or a dog. Would she never be safe from these slips?

'It's time Edward was put to his lessons,' said Christina. 'He's wilful, and says he won't study. Our good mother and I have both tried to teach him his letters, and both given up for the moment. But if you would work with him, Alys, perhaps he would try.'

'I should like that,' said Alys instantly. 'I shall ask our honoured parents.' She winked saucily at Jossey, and Jossey almost laughed.

So Alys joined Edward in lessons. One of Sir Philip's clerks, a cheery young man called Hubbard, took on the job of teaching them. The wayward Edward sulked and wouldn't attend to Hubbard; so matters ended with Hubbard teaching Alys and Alys teaching Edward later in the day. Edward had formed a strong attachment to Alys: she was still a novelty, and she helped to fill the gap left by the absent Humfrey. Alys was used to being left in charge of Rose, and desperately needed an outlet for the demonstrative part of her nature which the Castells never called for. She gave Edward rough cuddles, told him endless stories, romped with him when they were alone, and sang to him when he was tired.

In fact, Alys sang to the whole company. Sometimes, after dinner, when they were in the solar and it was hard to sew by draughty candlelight, Sir Philip would call for music. Christina, Annora and Jossey could all play the vielle and psaltery (kinds of violin and zither), after a fashion, but Alys didn't think their music up to Roger and Hawkyn's, and wished the Castells sang. One night when Christina had a sore finger and Jossey a headache and Annora was tired of playing, Alys offered to sing. She found the Castells didn't know her country songs; and, as she left out any improper ones, they enjoyed them as something fresh and innocently entertaining.

When Sir Philip was away, as he often had to be (often in Greenwich, where his ships were berthed), the evenings were even quieter. There were games to play — chess and draughts and backgammon — but these all meant sitting still; moreover, Lady Annis was bored by them. After a time Alys plucked up courage and taught the three older girls, and Edward, some of the singing and dancing games that had been the Butlers' evening entertainment in their hall. It was a bit slow, with so few dancers, but it was a pastime; and sometimes Mabell, Lady Annis's waiting-woman, or one or more of the other maids, were allowed to join in. Lady Annis approved, and sat watching, tapping a foot and sometimes helping to sing the tune.

There was one game she would never watch, though. Alys was not allowed to teach the others the ring-game which sounded as though it were about roses but which was actually about the Great Pestilence — the plague from which people might suddenly drop dead after hardly a sneeze. 'It's nothing to make a game about,' said Lady Annis, pinching her lips together, and Alys knew better than to disobey.

As if to make up for banning this game, Lady Annis taught them a wedding-game she had learned as a girl in the north country. Alys liked its music and its refrain, 'The lily, the rose, the rose I lay'; but she felt the bewilderment of the young girl in the song, married too soon, and thought always of Sisely and Pentecost as she sang 'How should I love, and I so young?'

'At Christmas, we could go down to the hall and teach the clerks and apprentices,' Alys suggested, greatly daring.

'As to that, I doubt whether Sir Philip would like it,' said Lady Annis, anxiously. 'It might turn into a vulgar romp.'

A vulgar romp was just what Alys would have liked; but she said no more. Perhaps Humfrey would be an ally, when he came home. Would he be more Butler — his original nature remaining; or more Castell — brought up among these still, concealing people, who kept their thoughts and emotions to themselves?

In spite of all these diversions, she found the sameness of life in the Castell household hard to bear. At Lordship Butlers there had been all the bustle of the farm; here, when Sir Philip's clients came, he saw them in the parlour attached to his counting-house, in the wing of the house in which the gatehouse stood. The family saw nothing of them unless they came to dinner. Mabell and the other servants were so quiet they were hardly noticeable. The family saw little of the clerks, either, although most of them lived in the house. Alys and Edward did have their lessons; but the three elder girls had finished their education (they could read, and speak French) and their only occupation, their 'work', was sewing — embroidery as well as the making of clothes and the hemming of sheets. They didn't spin, like the Butler girls, or weave like the Butlers' Spinney household. Neither did they cook. They were ladies.

Alys shocked them by knowing about simple cookery, and preserving, and by efficiently making a posset to soothe her mother's headache or a rub to ease her father's aching back. The users of Alys's country cures were grateful, all the same, and Alys got a little of her own back by teasing her sisters that they would never know if their cooks or stewards were cheating them, when they were housewives, if they didn't know how things were made. Annora and Jossey would shrug, but Christina at times became cross and depressed. Christina was betrothed, to Rayner Ballaster, one of her father's business acquaintances, a rich wine-merchant. He was a widower, and already over forty, and Alys could not help seeing that Christina dreaded rather than longed for her marriage.

The girls and Edward seldom went out, and this was hardest of all to Alys. It seemed to her that London must be the most exciting place in the world, teeming with people and packed with entertainments. The height of activity in Harlton had been market-day, apart from the summer dancing and the Christmas games and a few other celebrations at other times of year. The real high spot of everyone's life was a fair, when one came to Cantebridge: the fairs had a wonderful variety of things to buy and things to eat, and sometimes acrobats and musicians to watch and listen to.

London was like a perpetual fair. You could buy rich clothes, or rich spices, or books (all written by hand), or precious stones, or noble horses, every day if you knew where to go (Cheapside for clothes, Smithfield for horses, and so on); you could buy hot food at all hours from the shops in Cooks' Row, not far from Swan Lane. Alys wanted to go everywhere, taste everything, touch everything, and ask incessant questions; but she soon learned that a Castell didn't behave like this.

There was a church in a road near to Swan Lane, St Martin's, and they all went together to Mass several times a week. The congregation, men and women alike, eyed each other's clothes with interest and sometimes envy, but there was not much conversation after the service. Alys was glad her family were properly-behaved Christians, and impressed by how often they went to church. Harlton church didn't have Mass every day. There were shopping-trips, too, with Lady Annis and her children proceeding ceremoniously in her 'whirlicote' or town carriage — the first horse led, of course, and the progress painfully slow.

Apart from these expeditions, the children played ball, or battledore and shuttlecock, decorously in the garden, or walked in the cleaner of the neighbouring streets with a servant in attendance. Alys wanted to walk down to the river (Swan Lane ended in steps down to the water, Swan Stairs, and a little landing-stage for the small boats of the watermen who took passengers up and down the Thames), but Lady Annis would never allow that.

London Bridge, not far from where Swan Lane came out on the river bank, was a place of great fascination: a dramatic structure with nineteen arches, a drawbridge and gates to keep invaders from south of the city out. Houses stood on either side of the road which crossed it, and there was constant busy traffic, and a thoroughly enjoyable mix-up of riders, walkers, carts and carriages, with frequent minor accidents: Lady Annis thought it a most unsuitable place for young daughters.

Even nearer home, there were often street fights and shouting-matches between gangs of boys from different trades, and between Londoners and young people from the Flemish community. The Londoners resented these innocent but prosperous foreign weavers (who they felt had taken jobs which should have gone to Englishmen), and children would shout after them and their families in the street,

'Flemish fleas
Bandy knees
Can't
Say
Bread and cheese!'

'Why can't they?' Alys asked Mabell (who sometimes walked with the girls) the first time she heard this.

'God gave them clumsy tongues. They just can't pronounce it,' said Mabell.

'I don't suppose you and I could pronounce Flemish,' said Alys, and Mabell looked displeased.

Alys would have liked to watch open-air plays and the

games played in the various open spaces (except those where animals — sometimes poor old shambling bears and desperate badgers — were attacked and killed by packs of dogs). She loved seeing football played in the fields north of Thames Street. She would have liked to turn the Castells' ball-games into pig-in-the-middle or 'Who's got the ball?', but the older girls thought these too rough or too noisy, and Alys was continually being discouraged from running everywhere.

'Alys, Alys — we are ladies! Do remember,' Christina or Annora would say. Alys thought with a sort of homesickness of hawking with the boys around Lordship Butlers; racing their stocky ponies through the thistles; dancing the wild village farandoles with Sampson and Emm. She sometimes caught a gleam in Jossey's eye which seemed to say that Jossey, too, was not altogether convinced of the benefits of being a lady.

Still, Alys did have new clothes. Lady Annis thought her Harlton homespun too coarse, and her peace dress too thin, for late autumn; and gowns were made for her in scarlet and blue which filled her with delight — especially the scarlet. She had new shoes, too, in leather soft enough for gloves, and a silver chain for her neck. She longed to be able to show herself to Ede Butler, and to Maud and Rose and Emm.

When Mitchell, the servant who attended the girls on their walks, was sent off to Hatley, life became even more quiet. Nobody else could be spared to go with them, and they went no further afield than the garden. Alys watched Mitchell ride off, with longing in her eyes: he would be so close to Harlton.

'Why does he have to go?' she asked Annora, who was also watching.

'He has orders from our honoured father, for Master Cheeseman,' said Annora. 'To do with the farm, I think — cattle to be slaughtered and trees to be cut down. And he will bring the Christmas poultry back with him. We kill our own geese and capons for the great feasts.'

'It must be near now, then,' said Alys. 'And Humfrey will come.' She wished that he had been there in time for her birthday, which only Lady Annis had remembered and which had not been celebrated in any way (no Butler romps for her that year).

It seemed long, though it was under a week, until Mitchell returned. He came back with a farm cart loaded with coops of live, angry geese and drooping capons, the corners filled with good sweet logs of apple and pear which would burn clear on the big Christmas fires. And he had a message for Alys. As Lady Annis and her cook fussed over the fowls, and the carter Hob fussed over his horses, Mitchell drew Alys aside.

'I've a word for you, Mistress Alys,' he said.

'Who from?' asked Alys eagerly.

'Mistress Ede Butler sends you her kind remembrances, and tells you not to forget you are the Peace Child,' said Mitchell.

'Oh Mitchell — Mitchell!' said Alys, deeply delighted. 'Did you see her?'

'No, no, not her,' said Mitchell. 'I met a young man in the street in Hatley: he rode a grey horse and said he was a law-clerk in London. He told me.'

'Jordan!' said Alys, more pleased still. It must be Jordan, and this was a double contact with the Butlers.

Alys suddenly realized that Jossey was standing close and might hear their conversation.

'What happened to Jack Carter, Mitchell?' she said. 'Who drove away with my money?'

'He never went back to Hatley,' said Mitchell. 'He's not been heard of.'

'What is it, Mitchell?' Lady Annis called sharply, turning away from the problems of the cook. 'What's your news?'

'I called at Lord Osbern's manor as I returned, madam,' said Mitchell with a formal bow. 'Things were all in a hustle there and his lordship about to set out for Westminster. They must have been close behind me on the road, and I would guess Master Humfrey should reach here this afternoon.'

Lady Annis, and Jossey — and Alys, for a different reason — were all overjoyed. Her mother sent Jossey running indoors with instructions about Humfrey's bed, and Alys running to the kitchen with an order about pigeon pie — Humfrey's favourite — for dinner. Alys was pleased that Humfrey had such a fuss made over him.

She determined to see him arrive, and hung about the garden until daylight faded and her hands and feet grew too cold to bear. Dinner was being delayed, and Sir Philip beginning to be short-tempered; so Alys went up to the solar and occupied herself in playing with Edward there.

The commotion of Humfrey's arrival must have been heard all over the house. It sent Edward scuttling down the stairs to welcome his brother, and fetched all the family out of unexpected corners. Alys hung back, suddenly uncertain, and so she observed Humfrey from the top of the stairs, as Jossey had watched her, all those weeks ago.

A tall, handsome boy — but staggeringly tall, surely two or three inches taller than Jossey — he laughed and joked as he came in, flinging off his cloak. And then he peeled off his furry hat and bent to kiss his father's and his mother's hands — and Alys stared, clutching the stair-rail, transfixed with shock. Humfrey's bare head in the candlelight shone pale, pale gold, almost the silvery flaxen of Edward's. He was a Castell of the Castells.

Alys did not remember, afterwards, how she got down the stairs: she somehow found herself at the bottom, and being introduced to Humfrey in the general babble of rejoicing.

'What, another sister!' said Humfrey, in mock-horror; but he kissed her warmly. 'Hey, I've seen you, though,' he added.

'Yes, and I've seen you,' said Alys. 'But where?'

'You were the little singer-girl, who came with the minstrels,' said Humfrey. 'I thought at the time you looked just like Jossey. The ladies talked about you for days afterwards.'

'I did travel with minstrels,' said Alys. 'I remember now — in the great hall, you were one of the pages waiting on the high table. Think — if you'd said to me "You look like my sister", we might have got to know each other then.'

'I wasn't thinking about much except my dinner,' said Humfrey. 'It was cold, too. All that music took an age.'

'So that grand house was our uncle's,' Alys said with pleasure. 'I did enjoy our uncle's food, even though it was coolish.'

'Osbern always did himself well,' said Sir Philip. 'And now our lost sheep has arrived, we can go to our own dinner. Wash your hands, Humfrey my son, and come to table.'

Dinner was a lively meal. Humfrey was only staying one night at Ship House and then going on to Westminster to join Lord Osbern; his parents encouraged him to talk and to tell them all the gossip of the Osbern household. Lord Osbern was not Humfrey's uncle by blood: he was the brother of Sir Philip's first wife (mother of Harry and Robert), who had been dead for many years. He seemed to be a popular uncle with the family; and his mother, Lady Katherine, had sent purses with gold coins in them for each of the Castell children. There wasn't one for Alys but Christina, seeing her downcast look, gave her her own.

'I shan't need this, Alys,' she whispered. 'I shall be married in the spring and have a rich husband to give me purses.'

Alys gave her a surreptitious kiss. A purse with money in it was a marvellous novelty to her.

During dinner, Alys hardly took her eyes off Humfrey's face and hardly noticed what she was eating. He could not, not possibly, be anything other than a Castell by birth and blood: where was the other Peace Child?

As so often, she went to Christina for help. Christina was embroidering a belt for Humfrey and went away after dinner to finish it in secret. Alys slipped off after her and crouched beside her in the pool of light from one candle.

'Christina,' she said. 'Please tell me. I thought Humfrey was a Butler child — the one exchanged for me. But he isn't, is he?'

Christina put her sewing down. 'My poor Alys,' she said. 'I thought you knew all about it. Humfrey is pure Castell. He's Jossey's twin.'

'Jossey said he was younger than she,' said Alys.

'He is — about twenty minutes,' said Christina. 'She used to tease him about it, but she's stopped now he's so tall.'

'And the other child — the Peace Child?' urged Alys.

'The Peace Child was called Thomas,' said Christina. 'In the outbreak of the plague five years ago, three little boys of this family died: Thomas, and John and Robin who were twins.'

'I see,' said Alys, suddenly understanding the importance of Humfrey and Edward, and why Edward might be spoiled.

'Thomas was a lovely child,' said Christina. 'He was dark, of course, and rosy, and full of love and fun and naughtiness. He used to sing: before he could talk he would sing. He was my favourite.' Tears gathered in Christina's eyes, and Alys scrambled up and hugged her. 'Don't cry, Christina, don't,' she said. 'You'll spoil your sewing.'

But she cried herself, in the dark night when Christina was asleep, silently, her tears soaking the bolster. For Thomas, a loving scamp of a child, dead without knowing his own mother; and for Ede Butler, who had parted with a baby son and who did not know that he was dead. She fell asleep at last in the deep small hours, knowing what she must do. She must go back, and tell Ede Butler the truth, and offer her back her substitute child. 'Don't forget you are the Peace Child,' Ede had said.

It would not be Christina who would help her now. In the dark morning, before breakfast was eaten and the family went to Mass, Alys caught Jossey on her own. She found her combing tangles out of her hair when the other girls had gone downstairs.

'Jossey,' said Alys. 'Help me, please. I want to go back.'

'Why?' said Jossey, staring.

'Because Thomas is dead,' said Alys. 'Thomas is dead, and I didn't know. I have to tell my mother.'

'Your foster-mother,' said Jossey (but kindly, now).

'My first mother,' said Alys. 'I can't tell Sir Philip and Lady Annis I'm going. I can't tell anyone, or I'd be stopped. Except you. Will you help?'

'If you really mean it,' said Jossey. 'Yes, I'll help.'

Instead of relief, Alys felt desolation. Her feelings were too near the surface to be hidden now, and she said, 'Do you dislike me so much, Jossey? Do you want me gone?'

Jossey put out a hand towards her and almost touched her. 'I don't dislike you at all, Alys,' she said. 'When you came, I suddenly felt old. That I'd soon be betrothed to a man I hardly knew, like Christina; and that I wanted time to stop, and myself still to be the youngest girl. None of that was your fault. And I did think you were half a villein! You brought us fun, though, and I'll be sorry when you're gone. But you can't exist not knowing who you are. Our honoured parents let you go to be a Butler, and neither they nor you can just blot that out.'

'I want to be both,' said Alys, 'Castell and Butler. But I have to go, because of Thomas.'

'Hob will take the farm cart back to Hatley today,' said Jossey. 'Master Cheeseman needs it on the farm. The empty poultry-coops will be on it. You could hide. Put your old grey dress on, though, and your cloak: that scarlet will get itself seen.'

'It will take a farm cart three days,' said Alys. 'Shall I survive?'

'Why not?' said Jossey. 'The weather's mild. You can take bread, and I'll fill you a bottle of water and wine.'

Alys pleaded a headache, and didn't go to Mass. Her heavy and puffy eyes, and weary look, bore out her story.

'Too much excitement,' said her father. 'Well, you don't get a new brother every day. Stay by the fire, Alys, and say your prayers here. Mind you remember.'

While the Castell family were at Mass, the farm cart left for East Hatley. Two of the empty poultry-coops had been pulled together, and lying inside them, covered by a couple of sacks, was Alys. She had a loaf of bread and a hunk of cheese, wrapped in a napkin; and a stoppered bottle, too full to swish. She was cold and cramped and miserable, and she longed to kiss her family goodbye and explain herself properly, but she knew better than that. The Castells had taken her as their own, and maybe even took some pride in her: they would not be inclined to let her go.

That first day's journey was a dreadful day for Alys. The cart was an open one and she didn't dare to get right out of her coops, for fear of attracting Hob's attention. It might be inevitable for Hob to see her, but if this did happen it must be when it was too late for him to turn back, and his only course would be to take her on to Hatley. A couple of times Hob stopped at small alehouses and left the cart beside a hedge; Alys could slip out to relieve herself and stretch her stiff joints. But she was too afraid of being noticed to stay for long out of her hiding-place. She looked forward to darkness; but not to the increasing cold as night came on. How could she manage if the night brought crackling frost, or driving rain which would blow into her sketchy shelter?

Her luck was in. Hob stopped for his night's rest at a tavern in Barkway, and Alys, peering out from her sacks, saw that the courtyard of the inn was full of lights and a jostle of travellers — horses, luggage-carts, and a long travelling-carriage for ladies. The travellers themselves were dismounting and disembarking from the carriage, and Alys, overjoyed, noticed the glitter of badges on their hats and the fact that they had a priest with them, in black gown and clerical haircut. This time she really had found her pilgrims.

Hob was indoors, and Alys scrambled from the cart and made straight for the priest. He was a much-travelled pilgrim, hung about with pendants and little bottles containing the blood of saints.

'Father,' said Alys, clutching at his sleeve, 'are you pilgrims?'

'Certainly, child,' said the priest. 'We are bound to the shrine of Walsingham, twenty-five souls of us.'

'And will you halt at the shrine of Our Lady of White Hill in Haslingfield?' asked Alys.

'Yes, indeed,' said the priest. 'We should be there by midday, the day after tomorrow.'

'May I ride with you to White Hill?' said Alys. 'I haven't got a horse, but I've got a gold coin and I can pay my way. I'm going to my foster-family at Lordship

Butlers. I'm travelling with a carter but I don't trust him, and I'd rather go with you.'

'Lordship Butlers, eh?' said the priest. 'Then you know the good priest of Harlton.'

'Sir William Tele taught my foster-brothers Latin,' said Alys eagerly. 'Hugh and Ede Butler, and Sir Steven, will be grateful if you let me go with you.'

Alys didn't realize that by producing the names she had passed the careful priest's test. He nodded briefly, and said, 'You are welcome. Hire a horse if you choose, but there's room and to spare in the carriage. You can pay your share of the carriage-hire.'

And so Alys journeyed to Haslingfield with the holy pilgrims, sharing a bed on the first night with a young woman going to pray for the recovery of her ill husband and who cried in the night; and on the second with a stout lady who was carrying out a penance and who was as warm as a stove but snored alarmingly.

The pilgrims travelled slowly, stopping for prayers at all the larger of the wayside shrines and singing hymns at some of them. They ate well, and the ladies' carriage, although the seats in it were only backless benches, was the most comfortable conveyance Alys had ever been in. She joined heartily in the songs and prayers, and paid her groat whenever money was called for. Many of the prayers she said were for the kindly Dame Katherine and Christina, whose joint gift of money stood her in such good stead. Some were for the soul of Thomas Butler, and for her foster-mother Ede.

Alys found the conversation of the ladies in the carriage not as altogether holy as she had expected, laughed at their jokes, and was quite sad to think her journey with them would be short. They were all Londoners, and she didn't think she would be likely ever to meet them again.

The cavalcade wound its way back through the places Alys knew, and in good time she warned the priest about the hermit by the bridge.

'I know about her, daughter,' he said. 'A poor mad soul. We shan't stop at her hut.'

And indeed they didn't: they hurried past at a sharp trot, throwing her a shower of small coins as she held up begging hands. Alys pulled her hood across her face and avoided the hermit's eyes, remembering her misery in that smoky hut.

At noon on the third day they sighted White Hill, and Alys began to sweat slightly with excitement and fright. A wind had got up, and when the company converged on the shrine, high on the chalky hillside, their skirts and cloaks and the liripipes of their hoods blew like wild banners. The song in praise of Mary which they sang was blown out of their mouths and hardly audible.

Alys sang with them, giving thanks for her safe return, and afterwards said her goodbyes to her fellow-travellers.

'We shall meet in heaven,' said the fat lady piously, giving Alys a hearty kiss.

'Will you be all right on foot?' asked the priest. 'This is a gale and a half.'

'I shall be all right,' Alys assured him. 'I know the road. This is my home.'

She turned and ran, into the teeth of the wind — the westerly which she knew so well. The pilgrims' farewell shouts were blown away and she hardly heard the rattle of the carriage and the carts.

She couldn't run all the way: it was two miles of track and road, and not much of a road underfoot — holed and muddy. She soon slowed down, with a stitch in her side, and took a compulsory rest behind a tree to avoid a passer-by (Kit, the blacksmith's son, leading a newly-shod horse). As soon as she reached the first cottages of Harlton she began to run again, and nobody had stopped her — or as far as she knew, recognized her — when she got to Emm's.

Emm was alone in the cottage, kneading dough at the one table. She stopped when she saw Alys, and raised her sticky white hands to her face in shock.

'Is it really you, Alys?' she whispered. 'Not a ghost?'

'It can't be a ghost, you goose, Emm,' said Alys vigorously. 'I'm not dead, am I? I went to London.'

'We heard you'd never come back,' said Emm. 'That you found you'd got grand relations, and you chose them instead of us ordinary people.'

'I had to know about them — that's why I went,' said Alys. 'And I've come back, haven't I?'

'So I see,' said Emm. 'But Mistress Butler told me you were really one of the Castells, and had gone to live with them.'

'I meant to,' said Alys. 'Emm, will you go and tell my mother? I want to see her first, on her own, not all in a muddle with everybody talking at once. Will you run to Lordship Butlers, and fetch her here?'

'All right,' said Emm. 'When I've set the dough to rise.'

Alys sat, as patient as she could, while Emm set the dough in its flat pan at the side of the hearth. Then Emm flung her torn cloak around her shoulders, slid her feet into clogs, and ran off bareheaded across the fields by the muddy path. Alys slipped off her own hood, smoothed her rough hair, and spread her hands to the fire to warm her chilled fingers. The Baxters' cat crept in and crouched near her feet.

When Alys heard feet running, and one pair of feet alone, she was afraid that Emm had returned without Ede Butler. But it was Ede herself, running to the cottage, her cloak flung on hastily over the apron she hadn't stopped to take off, her indoor cap still on her head. Emm had lagged behind, and Alys was grateful. Her one wish was to see her foster-mother alone.

'Alys, Alys!' panted Ede at the door, holding out her arms. 'Are you well? Do you choose us after all? What is it, chuck?'

Alys clung to her, burying her face in the apron which smelt of flour and honey and home.

'Oh, mother, I had to come back. I had to tell you,' she said. 'You see, it's Thomas. Thomas is dead.'

Ede Butler rocked Alys back and forward, holding her close against herself, and as Alys's tears soaked her apron, Ede's fell on Alys's head.

'Don't cry so, my lamb, my coney,' she said. 'Would I part with a child and think no more about it, and ask no more about its doing badly or well? You are welcome back, Alys, for whatever reason. But of course I knew Thomas was dead.'

'But how did you know? Who told you?' Alys asked, as the two went hand-in-hand towards Lordship Butlers.

'The Castells have a man, Hob, on their Hatley farm,' said Ede Butler.

'I know him,' interrupted Alys. 'He drives a cart.'

'He has a sister in Harlton, Meggot the smith's wife,' said Ede. 'I asked her to give me news whenever she had it, and she did. I did my mourning for Thomas five years ago.'

'Two other little boys died,' said Alys. 'But Christina liked Thomas best. She cried when she told me.'

'Then you have a kind sister,' said Ede.

'They're all kind,' said Alys. 'In their way.'

'You have a lot to tell us,' said Ede. 'But it can wait. You must go to your grandfather first.'

'Oh dear,' said Alys. 'Will he beat me?'

'I shouldn't be surprised,' said Ede. 'Ask yourself whether you've deserved it. We hunted the countryside for you. For a week we thought you were dead, until the messenger with Sir Philip's letter came. We expected to find your corpse in every ditch. There were prayers and tears and agonies. You ought to have thought of that, my Alys, before you left like that.'

There was a great outcry in the hall of Lordship Butlers when Ede came in with Alys, but Ede hushed them all and hurried Alys off to Sir Steven. He was sitting alone in his parlour, where a small fire in a brazier kept the cold from his arthritic leg, and he was reading a tiny book of prayers, holding it close to his face because the lettering was so minute.

'What's this — the Peace Child!' he said, abruptly lowering his book. 'Why have you come back to us, Alys?' His face was stern.

Alys knelt and kissed his hand. 'Sir,' she said, 'because Thomas is dead.'

'Did it take you three months to find that out?' asked Sir Steven. 'Stand up, child, and speak clearly. Don't snuffle. You can leave us, Ede. I'll sort this out.'

'Well, it did,' said Alys. 'I thought Humfrey was the Peace Child, but this week he came home and he's as pale as a primrose. So I asked.'

'I see,' said Sir Steven. 'And what made you go off there like an arrow from a bow, without a word to anyone?'

'I found out who I was,' said Alys. 'I made Pentecost tell me. It wasn't her fault — I dragged it out of her. And I felt I had to go and see them, and see what it meant to be a Castell.'

'And what did you think of them, in the end?' asked Sir Steven.

Alys launched into her answer without hesitation; and once she had got started she talked on like a flowing stream. How the Castells were kind, and had welcomed her; were quiet, an orderly uneventful household; were proud and reserved; were — in the case of Edward — wilful.

'So who, now, do you think you are?' asked Sir Steven finally, eyeing her keenly. 'You see, Alys, this has a familiar ring to me. Proud and wilful and reserved might add up to a child never known for her good temper; a child who could hatch a drastic plan without a word to anyone; a child determined to do as she wanted quite regardless of others and their feelings.'

'You mean I'm a Castell, and should go back to them,'

said Alys. 'But if I do, shan't I just get worse? Maybe the Butlers are what I need, to laugh at me and tease me and scold me and love me so that I can grow like them.'

'Well argued,' said Sir Steven. 'And possibly true.'

'And if I was wrong not to tell anyone I was running away, so I think were you all wrong not to tell me who I was,' said Alys, suddenly bold (and expecting to be beaten, anyway).

'We should have remembered you were a Castell, and likely to behave like one, do you mean?' said Sir Steven. 'Well, perhaps. I don't think our treatment of you was altogether wise. But it was loving.'

'I know,' said Alys. 'And the Castells love me, too, which makes it harder. I thought Jossey didn't like me, at first, but I found she didn't mind me at all. Oh, grandfather, what will you do? Will you send me back?'

'Legally, I should,' said Sir Steven. 'Are you telling me you want to stay? The Castells are rich by comparison with us: they can do much for you — make you a fine marriage.'

'It's my mother,' said Alys. 'I mean my Butler mother. I love you all, but with her it's different and special. I didn't realize until I went away. I was never really comfortable, away from her.'

'She rocked you and cradled you when you were a babe in arms,' said Sir Steven. 'Ede always liked to have more to do with her babies than the nurse did, though you all had careful nurses as a gentleman's children should. I would say she loved you like her own baby, but perhaps she loved you more; and does. Perhaps she feels you need it.'

'I do,' said Alys.

'I said, don't snuffle,' said Sir Steven. 'Put your hand on my prayer-book and swear in the name of God that you will never again run off without a word.'

The little prayer-book lay flat on his open hands. Alys put hers over it and repeated the promise.

'Now that's an oath,' said Sir Steven. 'I shall write to Sir Philip and say you are here, and nothing more. He must take the initiative, if he wants you back. And if he does, I can hardly hold you.'

'And I suppose you'll beat me,' said Alys with a sigh. Sir Steven's walking stick was conveniently at hand.

'I doubt I have the right to,' said Sir Steven. 'And you the child of the Castells! You will have to behave yourself without beating. You are the Peace Child.'

Alys hugged him — a proper Butler hug, with a lot of squeeze — and escaped full of joy to kiss and cuddle and shout with her Butler brothers and sisters. And talk, and talk, and talk.

What they wanted most to hear about, to her surprise, was Harry Brag and Robert.

'I didn't see either of them,' said Alys, to universal disappointment. 'Harry is in Westminster, and Robert is in London learning law.'

'I knew that,' said Nicholas, who had just come in from the stables. 'Jordan said so. He has a bad name there: they call him Robert Fox.'

'God help the laymen, when the lawyers are so wild,' said Gilbert.

'Harry and Robert's mother died when they were tiny boys,' said Alys. 'I suppose Sir Philip spoiled them. He didn't spoil me: I had to behave properly.'

'Do they have fine clothes?' asked Rose.

'Oh, yes,' said Alys with enthusiasm. 'I had new dresses, red and blue; but I left them behind.'

'And a fine house?' asked Maud.

'In some ways,' said Alys. 'It has an inside staircase, and an inside privy, called a garderobe. And glass in the windows.'

'Use your eyes, Alys,' said Sisely, laughing. 'So have we.'

'A travelling glazier came soon after you went, and all the main windows are done,' said Ede, looking up from her spinning.

'So they are,' said Alys. 'The Castells' glass is clearer than ours, but ours is prettier.' She liked the greenish colour, and the swirls and bubbles in it.

'Tell what happened on the road — how did you travel?' asked Maud and Walter at once; and Alys was launched on a story that went on so long that Ede stopped her and took her off to the kitchen to make pastry.

'That's enough from you, Alys,' she said firmly.

'Yes, mother Butler,' said Alys. 'And I'm running out of voice.'

But the telling of her story didn't end with the people at Lordship Butlers. Alys had to visit Butlers' Spinney and retell it all to Uncle Richard, Aunt Joan and her cousins. Jordan was at home on a visit and he laughed more than anyone at the comic parts of Alys's adventures, and insisted on several repeats of her encounter with Sir Baldwin St George. 'The old scoundrel,' he said each time. 'That man thinks he's outside the law.'

There was only one week to go till Christmas, and Alys was at once sucked into all the preparations.

'How glad I am to be having Christmas here!' she whispered to Maud in bed at night.

'Don't you really want to go back? To a house like that, and new dresses, and your own real mother and sisters?' asked Maud.

'I want both,' said Alys. 'But Christmas will be nicer here.'

She enjoyed Christmas with especial vividness; most of all the singing and dancing games in the hall, with all the household; tugs-of-war; and kisses, under the kissing-bough, to be paid as forfeits. The Lord of Misrule (a part played by John Atwater, the bailiff) kept things humming, and ended Twelfth Night with an all-night party for which the whole family — and it seemed, half the village — stayed up, and there was no pause in the songs and dances and rough fun. Sir Philip would have called it a vulgar romp, Alys supposed, and she savoured every minute of the twelve days.

Two things made it especially precious to her. One was that any day a message might come from Sir Philip, demanding her return. The other was that change was in the air: this was the last Christmas that all the Butlers would be together. Sisely was to be married in the spring, to Everett Haward of Ashwell. Hugh Butler grumbled a little, on the quiet, at how much the marriage was costing him: Everett had expected a large dowry. Alys wondered, anxious for a moment, who would pay a dowry for her.

Everett was a man in his late twenties, inclined to be noisy, and full of jokes; he came on a visit to his betrothed and brought a gift of game for the family and a jewelled girdle for Sisely. Sisely seemed to have made her mind up to like her husband, but there was a sad look about her sometimes. Alys wondered how many of her thoughts were still for Avery. Gilbert, although he was a farmer at heart, had decided to become a monk and so was studying at Cantebridge. He hoped he would end up working on the monks' land and perhaps managing some of their estates. A Norfolk landowner wanted to marry Julian, but Hugh Butler had not made up his mind about the terms. Julian was sewing herself new clothes as fast as she could, in case a rapid decision was reached — even if she did not get married for some time, there would be a betrothal ceremony. Walter felt left out of everything, and was grumpy and a bit on edge.

'How empty Lordship Butlers will be, when they all go!' Alys said to him one day, sighing over her spinning. 'I do wish things didn't have to change. I want to be a child for ever, and have Ede Butler for my mother.'

'You were the first to go,' said Walter, a bit sharp.

'I know,' said Alys. 'But I did come back.'

As the days went by, and no letter came from Sir Philip, Alys began to feel more settled. It was sad in a way that the Castells didn't make a fuss about her leaving them; it suggested they could do very well without her. But it was a relief beyond words that she could stay with the Butlers, and especially with Ede. She did her best to be a useful daughter, and often suppressed a quarrelsome answer: 'remember you are the Peace Child,' Ede had said, and her grandfather had said much the same. He didn't call her Lilyflower any more, but he watched her and treated her with a courteous kindness that pleased her but worried her too. Did it mean he no longer felt she was one of his family?

He took her on one side one day, and warned her against seeing too much of Emm.

'But she's my friend,' Alys objected. 'And her sister is one of our household.'

'I know that,' said Sir Steven. 'And very good people they are — all the Baxter kin. But they are villeins, Alys. You should think what your Castell family would feel about your friendship with Emm, not what your own feelings are. You know the Castells best. What would they say?'

'Oh dear,' said Alys. 'Why do changes have to be for the worse, and spoil things? Why is it all so unfair?'

'It's not a simple world,' said Sir Steven. 'If God had wanted to make it simple, and us, he could have done it. And he could have made it fair. He didn't; and we should probably still have been discontented, if he had.'

Alys went away gloomy. She still saw Emm, but their meetings were shorter and Alys chose another ear than Emm's to whisper secrets in. She spent more time with the Paunton girls than she had done before: plump little Maudlin, and her sisters, were not so much fun as Emm, but even the Castells would have agreed they were ladies.

When spring began to come, with snowdrops showing first through the February mud, Alys asked for her reading and writing lessons to be continued.

'If her parents set her to learn, she should learn,' said Ede Butler to Hugh.

It wasn't thought proper for Alys to go to the priest's house with the boys, so once a week Sir William came to Lordship Butlers and taught Alys and Maud (the other girls wouldn't be bothered), and in between times she practised with Walter. She bought herself a psaltery, too, from a pedlar, and taught herself to play — much teased by all the boys about her false notes and discords.

'If Jossey can, I can,' said Alys, and stuck to it.

There was lovely spring weather that year, the snow all gone by early February, and March bringing some sunny days when the children, sniffing the fresh windy air, chased about like spring lambs. The farm was busy, with real lambs being born, weeds sprouting up in every furrow and seed to be sown; and in the house, the girls all united to make Sisely's bridal clothes and to plan elaborate confections for her wedding. Alys was busy and happy and entirely content.

In late March the cowslip flowers came out, and Alys took on the job of harvesting them for the making of cowslip wine. The pastures between Lordship Butlers and the church and the rest of the village were full of them, a dancing pale gold shimmer over the grass. Time after time Alys went out and filled her rush basket as full as it would go.

Late one morning, as she was filling her apron preparatory to loading her basket up to its handle, she saw a stranger coming towards her along the footpath. He was big-built and heavy-shouldered, with a reddish face and a brown curly beard. Alys stood aside to leave him the path, but he stopped and spoke to her.

'Is this the way to Lordship Butlers?' he asked her.

'Yes,' said Alys. Girls didn't speak to strange men, but anyone should answer a civil question.

'And are you one of the Butler family?' asked the stranger.

'No, but I live there,' said Alys. 'I'm Alys Castell.'

'So I thought,' said the stranger, and without another

word he seized Alys, swinging her off her feet and kicking over her basket, and ran with her back towards the road. Alys yelled, loud as a squealing pig, but there was nobody about in the field or on the road, and nobody heard.

Behind a clump of trees was standing a light travelling carriage, the sort ladies used, with horses harnessed head-to-tail in front. A driver stood at the head of the front horse. Alys shrieked in good earnest when she saw this — was she to be kidnapped? Her captor pressed her face into his shoulder, to muffle the noise she made, and bundled her into the carriage, jumping in behind her. The driver was quickly up on his box, and the horses whipped and rattling fast away — past the Washpit, past Emm's cottage, and off towards the Roman road and London. Alys kicked and wriggled, but she did no good: she couldn't get free.

Only the overturned basket, and the spilt and scattered cowslips, showed that she had been taken away by force and had not gone freely, breaking her oath.

When at last they were well out of the village the man let go of Alys (except that he still gripped one wrist) and laughed at her.

'Shout your best now, Mistress Alys,' he said. 'When Castell meets Castell it's bound to be a battle; but the rule of war is generally that the biggest wins.'

'I know who you are, then,' said Alys. 'Harry Brag.'

Harry slapped her. 'Nobody uses that name to me,' he said fiercely. Alys bit the hand that held her wrist, and Harry slapped her again.

'Are you taking me to my parents?' Alys asked.

'Where else?' said Harry.

'Mind, then,' said Alys. 'They won't be best pleased if they get me back covered in bruises.'

'Shrew!' said Harry, and Alys knew what he meant, having been bitten herself by one of the little mouse-like creatures, with ferocious teeth, which she was trying to rescue from a cat. She didn't mind at all if Harry thought her spiteful. And for whatever reason, he didn't hit her again.

'Who told you to fetch me?' she asked Harry, when she judged his fit of temper had subsided. 'Sir Philip?'

'Nobody tells me,' said Harry. 'I choose what I do.'

'But does my father want me?' asked Alys.

'Our father said nothing,' said Harry. 'The one who spoke of you was the Lady Annis: she said over and over she wished you were there.'

'And so you decided to take me by force,' said Alys. 'Why didn't you just write to Sir Steven and ask for me?'

'What! Do you suppose he'd have let you go?' said Harry.

'Yes, for sure,' said Alys. 'I'm a Castell.'

'You don't know much,' said Harry. 'A Peace Child, aren't you. You know nothing at all about the way men think.'

Alys drew a breath to reply, but let it out again. 'When the Butlers next ask me what Harry Brag is like,' she thought to herself, 'I shall tell them he's a stuck-up windbag and a bore.' At the same time she wondered whether she would ever see another Butler.

There was no chance to attempt an escape: if there had been, Alys would have tried — as much to annoy Harry Brag as to avoid returning to the Castells. But Harry kept always a firm hand on her wrist. When the two men changed over for Harry to have a turn at driving, the first driver let the horses stand and came to the carriage door rather than give Alys a chance to make a dash for it. Alys thought the other man might make a pleasant change from Harry; but she was disappointed. The other man was Robert.

'Well, Mistress Alys,' he said when he was sitting beside her and had a good grip on her. 'How do you like your half-brothers?'

'Oh — are you Robert?' said Alys. She was careful, this time, not to use his nickname. 'I thought you were studying law.'

'I'm taking a vacation from the law,' said Robert. 'It's a dry old subject.'

'If you're not interested in it I suppose you won't know whether there's a law against stealing people,' said Alys.

'Abduction,' said Robert. 'What I'm doing to you isn't abduction. You're being returned to your own parents. You're their property, as much as if you were a sideboard.'

'Why does my mother want me back?' asked Alys.

'Just fancied having you: a sick fancy, I'd call it,' said Robert. 'She's going to have another child, in August (and that will put pretty little Edward's nose out of joint). Wanting a whinging white misery of a girl like you to keep her company is unaccountable any other way: she's got three already.'

Alys said no more. She wanted to ask all the family news but decided she'd prefer not to hear it from Robert. He was, she thought, the more odious of the two brothers: slighter and fairer than Harry but with a slyness of manner she especially disliked. She hoped against hope that Harry and Robert weren't living in Ship House now.

It was for her a horrible journey. Harry and Robert travelled fast — as fast as the still-muddy roads of spring allowed. March winds had put a dry crust on the mud, but it still lay thick underneath, waiting to bog down cartwheels and hooves and travelling feet. They made a few stops, at inns. Either Harry or Robert watched Alys all the while, and even stood outside when she visited the privy. At one inn they changed horses: they had hired horses here for part of the journey, and left their own in the stables to rest and wait for their return.

The nights were moonlit, so they travelled by night as well as by day. Sleeping was done in the carriage: whichever brother was not driving slept rolled in a blanket on the carriage floor, and Alys near him — tied to him wrist-to-wrist with a leather thong. Alys found this humiliating, but there was nothing she could do about it. She amused herself, and kept tears away, by imagining that she was Harry or Robert's dog, and that when she caught them one day in slippers and silk hose she would bite their ankles till the blood ran down. She carried these thoughts on into dreams, and ground her teeth in the short snatches of sleep the movement of the carriage allowed her. Once in the early light Robert pulled her awake.

'You grind your teeth like a dog,' he said. 'Fine wife you'll be.'

'In my dreams, I am a dog,' said Alys. 'My name is Holdfast, and I bite.'

Robert gave her a strange look, and Alys was pleased.

They got to Swan Lane early in the morning. Daylight had only just crept in, and only the servants were up in Ship House; but Sir Philip heard the horses, and came down in a dressing-gown, his hair ruffled up, to see who had arrived.

'Harry! Robert!' he said, agreeably pleased to see his sons, and 'In God's name, what's this?' as he caught sight of Alys.

'Lady Annis wanted her, so we fetched her,' said Harry.

'We knew you'd be glad,' added Robert, smiling his smooth smile. 'What pleases your lady wife must please you as well.'

'God have mercy, what have you done!' exclaimed Sir Philip. He seemed far from glad. 'Was there bloodshed?'

'No, nothing,' said Harry. 'I watched for the time. I took her picking flowers in a meadow; nobody knew.'

'What, no word to the Butlers — nothing?' said Sir Philip. 'Will you never learn we are at peace with them! Here, come with me; this needs some thinking about.'

He took his sons off to his parlour, and Alys heard as they went voices loud and angry and the words Butler and Castell frequently used. She felt glad that Sir Philip's ideas didn't match his sons', and that he was anxious to see the Butlers treated honestly; but she wished her father had spared time to make her feel a little welcome. Cold, dirty, hungry, and desperately tired, her old dress torn from the original scuffle with Harry, she stood in the hall and wondered if anyone in the world wanted her — except as a pawn in some game of their own invention.

Suddenly there was the flapping of bare feet running on the stairs, and Jossey, tangle-haired and wrapped in a sheet, came down in a rush, half-falling, and caught Alys in a real, close, Butler-like hug. Alys was almost too amazed to speak, but she hugged back as hard as she could.

'Alys! Alys!' Jossey said, in the middle of sobs: she couldn't get out any more words.

'It's all right, Jossey — I'm back,' said Alys. Annora, dressed as far as her shift, appeared at the top of the stairs, and she too ran down when she saw Alys. She seemed more concerned about Jossey than surprised to see Alys.

'I'm glad you're come,' she said to her. 'Help me with Jossey — we must get her back to bed.'

'But what is it — what's the matter?' whispered Alys. 'Is she ill? All this isn't on account of seeing me.'

'Didn't anyone tell you? Isn't that why you're here?' asked Annora. 'Humfrey is dead: he died at our uncle's, of smallpox. And Christina — Christina went to our uncle's on a visit. And she — well, she had the smallpox too.'

'But she's not dead? Not Christina?' begged Alys.

'No, no,' said Annora. 'Come along, Jossey, you can't stay in the hall in nothing but a bed-sheet.' She and Alys steered Jossey up the stairs between them, Jossey still crying into her curtain of hair and Alys scrabbling after the sheet-tails to try to prevent her tripping over them.

At the bedroom door Christina met them, and while Annora fussed over getting Jossey back into bed, Christina took Alys into her arms and kissed her and made her welcome. It was Alys's turn to cry now: not over Humfrey, or Jossey's grief for him, but over the pock-marks, some deeply-grooved and reddish, and others like the small stars that scatter the sky, that marked Christina's gentle face.

The womenfolk might be pleased to see her, but Alys was in her father's bad books. Sir Philip sent for her as soon as he had finished talking to Harry and Robert, beat her first, and asked for an explanation of her behaviour afterwards.

'I have acknowledged you as my child,' he said. 'Before the world I declared you to be a Castell. And you make me ridiculous by running off on a moment's notion, like a —' he hesitated for a simile '— a cow bitten by a gad-fly.'

Bruised as she was, in body and feelings, Alys had a job not to laugh at her mental picture of one of Hugh Butler's heifers off at full tilt across the pasture.

'Sir,' she said, 'the exchange of children was a bargain. When I left the Butlers and came to you, I was breaking the bargain. But Thomas is dead, and when I heard that, I didn't know who I was, Castell or Butler; I only knew Ede Butler had lost a child.'

'Well — and would it even the score to make your own mother lose one, too?' said Sir Philip. 'You talk like what you are — an ignorant girl who should be keeping quiet at home, obeying her father. You know nothing about the law. The contract between us and the Butlers was void when Thomas died.'

'Was it?' said Alys. She thought Sir Philip spoke with no great conviction. 'You didn't send for me then.'

'No, and neither did I send for you this week,' said Sir Philip sharply. 'Harry and Robert have vexed me severely, at a most unhappy time for this household. I've sent them about their business: your mother can do without any additional upsets, after losing a dear son. You had better behave yourself, too, now that God has sent you back to us. Go to your room and stay there.'

Alys went. She went, in fact, to bed, sharing the bed of Jossey who was being cosseted and given bread and milk by Christina. Alys was glad to wash thoroughly and comb her hair and climb into a warm bed; and she slept until Christina woke her at midday. Jossey was gone.

'Our honoured mother is asking for you,' said Christina. 'I've got you clean clothes, Alys. Do you feel refreshed?'

Alys did, and asked for her red dress. Christina helped her dress; and as she did Alys asked shyly, 'Christina — your wedding. Is it — when will it be?'

'In April, as planned,' said Christina. 'My father asked Master Ballaster if he wished to be free of the engagement, when I — when I came back from our uncle's like this. But he said he would honour it. He's a good man.'

'Then we must start to plan your wedding-dress,' said Alys. 'One of my Butler sisters will be married just before you. I'll tell you all about her clothes, though I know yours will be prettier.'

Christina's worn look cheered a little, and two fairly bright girls went together to Lady Annis in the solar. Lady Annis's welcome-back to Alys was full of reproaches, but a welcome it was; and Edward's was one of uncomplicated delight.

It was a gloomy house Alys had come back to. Many children died young, and many parents learned not to love too deeply, but Annis Castell had given her strongest feeling to her eldest son and Jossey's love for her twin had been her greatest secret, not much talked about but still the most vivid thing in her life. Annis seemed to be expecting her new child without any pleasure, and sat listless most of the day, her hands loose in her lap. Alys looked from her strained face to Jossey's, to Annora's inexpressive look (was she indifferent?) and Christina's marked cheeks and forehead. There was no comfort for her anywhere: no one who had the heart to ask her about her own griefs, and whether she missed Lordship Butlers and her other family there.

Alys couldn't bear the silence and heaviness of the house, Lady Annis often in tears by day and Jossey sobbing aloud at night. Fortunately Jossey's crying usually woke Alys up, and Alys grew used to cuddling her until she was quiet. A change of bed-partners took place and Alys shared with Jossey permanently, and Annora with Christina. Alys also told Jossey stories and wove imaginings about her future husband.

'When you get married, perhaps he'll be like Humfrey,' she said. 'Tall and fair and handsome, and he'll be called Sir Herriot Hendy.'

'Tell some more,' whispered Jossey, and Alys went on to invent Sir Herriot's exploits in war, his armorial bearings, the name of his destrier and his hawk and his faithful hound, and his fine clothes and armour. These stories were embroidered, night by night, and seemed to be genuinely comforting to Jossey.

To think of ways to console Lady Annis, or Christina, was harder; but Alys did what she could for them by making them plan and getting them busy about making things. Christina's trousseau became as absorbing a matter as Sisely's, and wrappers and cradle-sheets were stitched for the coming baby. Alys used her powers of invention to improve upon Sisely's clothes, and the baby-clothes Ede Butler would consider suitable, so that both Christina and the baby were lavishly over-provided for, in competition. It kept everybody hard at work, and little by little the family became less preoccupied with grief. In time Alys began to sing to them again.

She even discovered what was on the mysterious Annora's mind. Annora, now fourteen, was in a state of frantic trepidation as to whom Sir Philip would choose for her husband. Every time he brought a client home to dinner, or mentioned a colleague in conversation, Annora's mouth grew dry with fright. Would it be somebody old, like Christina's Master Ballaster, or somebody reasonably young and perhaps even good-looking? Alys wholeheartedly pitied Annora, and did the only thing she could to help. She invented a handsome husband for her, too, and Annora's Sir Evremond rivalled Jossey's Sir Herriot in glory. Annora said at times that the whole thing was unbelievably childish; but at others she egged Alys on to get another instalment of the story from her.

That summer, there was alarming news from the countryside; and Londoners who had country estates, like Sir Philip and Master Ballaster, muttered together in corners about their anxieties. From all over the east of England, from Kent up to Norfolk, there were rumours coming in to London of unrest among the farm workers, the 'villeins'. These men rented little pieces of land from the big landowners, and in return had to work for their overlords like slaves. The laws designed to keep them in their place — which said that they mustn't change jobs, or leave their home villages — were inflexible, and greedy landlords saw to it that life for many of these poor people was very hard. And now, they had a new tax to pay. The stories coming up to London told of trouble to come: agitators were stirring up the villeins to ask for rights and freedoms, and there was a smell of revolution in the air.

Sir Philip and Master Ballaster (who had a small manor in Essex) both went off to the country, and both came back reassured, telling each other that the stories were blown up out of all proportion and nothing was really wrong. Alys snooped on as many of their conversations as she dared, breathless to know whether or not the Castells would be going to Hatley in the summer. She had to admit to herself that things didn't look hopeful. There would be Christina to settle into her new home: there would be the new baby . . .

At least the rumblings from the manors didn't upset Christina's wedding. It seemed on the surface a happy enough affair. The feast was enormous, the dancing went on long enough to satisfy even Alys, and Sir Baldwin St George — though invited — didn't come. (Neither did any young man remotely like a Herriot or an Evremond.) Alys had yet another new dress, a deep rose-pink, and red leather slippers, soft as gloves; and walked behind her sister, important. Half her mind saw not St Martin's but the clean new church in Harlton; and she saw Sisely, as well as Christina, as a dignified and gently-smiling bride. Christina did her best to look happy; but Alys had noticed that the glances of fond pleasure which Rayner Ballaster had given her at one time, before her illness, were not the same now, but cooler, and that Christina was aware of this. Alys secretly believed that Sisely, with her boisterous Everett Haward, would be the happier of the two wives.

Christina's new house was in Suffolk Lane, only about ten minutes' walk from Swan Lane; and when Christina was settled there Alys was a frequent visitor. Once a week all the girls would go, and Lady Annis if she felt up to the walk; and once a week Christina and Rayner would come to dine at Ship House. But Alys slipped off every other day or so, in between needlework and lessons with Edward, and went with Mitchell in attendance, either on horse or on foot, to visit Christina on her own. She thought Christina's house dark and narrow, and intolerably dull; and although Christina talked cheerfully enough, and seemed busy about household affairs, Alys once or twice found her with wet cheeks.

'What is it, Christina?' she whispered once. 'Isn't he kind?'

'No, no, it isn't that,' said Christina, trying to smile. 'Not that at all. He's good and just. But oh, Alys, pray for me that I have a child; soon, soon! I must have something to love.'

So every visit, Alys stopped in St Martin's church on her way home, lit a candle and prayed for a child for

Christina (a son, she had decided, called Thomas). She enjoyed these calls in the church. Mitchell would wait outside for her. There was usually a group of women near the church door, met for a gossip out of the open air. Whispers and laughter ran around the group, and Alys liked the liveliness of it and the faint sense of conspiracy. None of their husbands could blame them for calling at the church for a prayer or two; none of their husbands was to know about the giggling that went on behind the door.

Another thing which Alys did off her own bat was to make a suggestion to Rayner Ballaster. Once after dinner she whispered to him while Sir Philip went for a flagon to fill his guest's wine cup (Sir Philip's wine was of a much finer quality since the marriage).

'Master Ballaster,' Alys hissed, and her brother-in-law jumped as if she had stung him.

'Well, Alys?' he said.

'Something I've thought of,' said Alys. 'If you want at any time to give Christina a present that will make her specially happy, give her a little dog.'

'Really?' said Rayner. 'Why?'

'She misses you when you are away from home on business,' said Alys, ready to invent a little in a good cause.

'Ah,' said Rayner. He looked interested. 'What sort of dog? A guard-dog?'

'More of a pet,' said Alys.

'Ah,' said Rayner again, and Alys sidled away as Sir Philip returned.

A month or so later Rayner presented Christina with two greyhound puppies, which became her great companions. She was profoundly grateful to him, and told him so often; and Alys hoped that the time of waiting for a child might be easier for both of them.

Although Alys's visits to Christina were accepted, her mother did sometimes complain at how very often Alys was missing from the house. So Alys took to slipping away unnoticed as often as she could, calling Mitchell from his other duties (or from standing about near the gatehouse waiting to let visitors in, and whistling horribly out of tune). One heavy, thundery June day, when the house oppressed her, Alys went for Mitchell as usual.

'Come on, Mitchell,' she whispered. 'I hate it in the house in this hot weather. I'm off to Mistress Ballaster's.'

'I don't know if I should leave my post today, Mistress Alys,' said Mitchell. 'I may be needed as a watchman. Rumour says that some of the villein rebels are in London, and are tearing houses like ours apart and cutting off their masters' heads in the street.'

'Oh, nonsense, Mitchell,' said Alys energetically. 'My father says that's all alarmist talk.' She thought of the villeins who were her friends, Emm and her family — and half Harlton. Surely these simple cheerful people would never gang up in mobs to tear houses apart. 'Come along,' she urged Mitchell. 'Sir Philip never actually said you must stay at your post, did he?'

'No,' Mitchell agreed unwillingly. 'He never said it in so many words. But at least, Mistress Alys, if you must go out, put your old cloak on over that scarlet dress. If there are rough characters about, at least we won't attract attention.'

Alys shot back to her room, and put on her old grey dress (uncomfortably small for her now) and tied a duster which she found on the stairs over her head like a kerchief. With her old thick shoes on her feet, she went back to Mitchell and made him a mock curtsy.

'I'm a poor country girl, and a stranger to London —' she began.

'Let's go at once, if we're going,' said Mitchell. 'Your cloak would have been better than that get-up.'

'Too hot,' said Alys. 'Nobody's in cloaks.'

They had hardly turned the corner out of Swan Lane (Mitchell walking like a good servant a few steps behind

Alys) when Alys hesitated and Mitchell cannoned into her.

'You're perfectly right, Mitchell,' said Alys. 'There are some funny people about. Look at those — they've all got some kind of weapon.'

'Bows,' said Mitchell. 'And long sticks. Ten to one it's the rebels.'

'Some have only got pitchforks,' said Alys. 'That won't get them far.'

'We must turn back, Mistress Alys,' said Mitchell with determination. 'You may be in danger.'

'Just to the church, Mitchell,' said Alys. 'They won't interfere with people going to church, and I must light my candle.'

Poor Mitchell was in a dilemma. It was no part of his job to contradict one of his master's family; but it was his job to protect Alys when she was out in the street. In the end he let her go, but insisted on walking beside her. He edged Alys towards the wall and walked outside her, looking apprehensively around.

'Don't look like that, Mitchell,' said Alys. 'Look casual and interested. Pretend you like the look of them.'

'But, Mistress,' groaned Mitchell, 'there's some of them round the church door, too!'

'Stop and talk to them while I go in,' urged Alys. 'Find out what they're doing and what they mean to do.'

'God save us all!' said Mitchell. 'I do believe I'm a coward.'

Alys gave the men grouped around the church door frankly curious looks, but in spite of her acting one of them still grabbed her by the elbow as she reached the door.

'What's your errand, mistress?' he asked.

'I'm going to say my prayers, good friend,' said Alys. 'For my —' she improvised rapidly — 'for my mother who is soon to have a child, and my sister who is newly married, and my good grandparents who are with the faithful departed, and my foster-grandmother —'

'Spare us your foster-grandmother!' exclaimed another man spitting. 'Get along in and be quick. You can have a little while — time for an "Our Father" or two.'

'All right,' said Alys. 'My brother will stay out here with you' (she gave Mitchell a saucy smile); 'send him to fetch me if I'm too long.'

She hurried into the church, went quickly for her candle and put it into the candle-stand where others were burning draughtily. When it was lit, and half-a-minute's worth of prayer quickly said, Alys looked around the church. The usual group of gossiping women was missing, otherwise the quiet shadowy place seemed its usual self. Or so she thought until she went to her favourite statue — St Martin himself, holding up half of his cloak, a brightly-painted wooden figure standing in a niche which was painted with a starry sky. It was the stars which attracted Alys; but today she could not see them all. Another figure, a living person, was sharing the niche with St Martin, half hidden behind the almost life-size saint. Alys stared, and stared again. She knew that skinny shape and that beaky nose — even skulking behind a statue in the half-dark.

'Sir Baldwin!' she whispered, too amazed to hold her tongue. 'Sir Baldwin St George!'

'For God's sake keep quiet!' muttered Sir Baldwin, with almost a groan. 'I've just a hope they don't know who I am.'

'What, the men outside?' asked Alys. 'So they know you're here?'

'Yes, the more's the pity,' said Sir Baldwin. 'They chased me here.'

'But you're safe here, anyway,' said Alys. 'It's sanctuary, isn't it. Nobody can touch you while you're in a church, even if you're a criminal, and all the law can do if it catches up with you is to banish you.'

Sir Baldwin laughed his short donkey's laugh. 'That's the theory,' he said. 'It's wasted on this lot. They've already dragged some people out from churches — from the very altars — and cut their throats.'

'Would they murder you?' Alys asked, staring again.

'I'm none too well-loved by my people in Hungry Hatley, girl,' said Sir Baldwin. 'They'd have my blood if they could. Wait, though!' he added, looking at her more closely. 'It's dark as the pit in here: but aren't you the Castell child?'

'We met,' said Alys demurely.

'And is your father anywhere near here?' asked Sir Baldwin.

'His house is,' said Alys. 'But he's out, I think.'

'Get a message to him, girl,' said Sir Baldwin, talking as though he was out of breath. 'Tell him I'm here. And that they're standing siege outside. They mean to sit it out till nightfall and drag me out in the dark.'

'But are you sure they're after you?' said Alys. 'If they don't know who you are?'

'Look at me!' groaned Sir Baldwin. 'In all my finery, out to woo a new wife. They'll have me for a rich swaggering oppressor of the poor, even if they don't know my name. It's even worse if they do. Get going, now!'

He certainly made an eye-catching sight, with gold chains around his neck, white fur on his green-and-gold doublet, and a ring on every finger Alys could see.

'Go on!' he urged her. 'It needs twenty or thirty men-at-arms, with swords and axes. That'll put paid to them. Tell Sir Philip — and at once.'

Alys ran for the door. But even as she went she thought, despairingly, that Sir Philip was undoubtedly out, and where was she to get twenty or thirty men-at-arms with swords and axes?

In spite of his fear, Mitchell seemed to be getting on well with the rebels at the door. He was telling them about a bear-baiting he had seen, and had got to the point where the bear had killed its fifth dog. Alys was glad the bear was holding its own, but interrupted without ceremony.

'Are you on that old story again, brother!' she said. 'Do come on, now — our dinner's waiting. I'm always hungry after I've said my prayers.'

'I suppose they got it in the end?' said one of the rebels.

'Tore it to pieces,' said Mitchell. 'Blood everywhere. Not enough of the skin left to make a good-sized hat.'

'Wish I'd seen it,' said the man, and Alys tugged at Mitchell's hand. The two of them went off at an easy walk, like people with no more thought than dinner waiting for them, and a mug or two of ale.

'Where did they come from?' said Alys as soon as they were out of earshot of the main group.

'Kent, mainly,' said Mitchell. 'Around Edenbridge and Cowden and that part. There's somebody pinned up in that church they don't mean to let go.'

'I know,' said Alys. 'I have to tell Sir Philip.'

'Let go my hand, now,' said Mitchell, embarrassed. 'We're near home.'

As soon as they were in Ship House Alys ran to the counting-house to ask for her father. He was in Greenwich, and the chief clerk, Master Arkwright, was in charge.

'Master Arkwright, we must act,' said Alys, as commanding as she could be. 'My honoured father's friend and landlord, Sir Baldwin St George, is trapped in St Martin's church by the rebels. They mean to have him out and murder him, and he says it needs twenty or thirty men-at-arms to get him out.'

Master Arkwright shook his head, wisely and sadly. 'We've no hope of getting help, mistress,' he said. 'News has just come in, by a servant of our neighbours, the Ardens, that the revolters are all over London and the soldiery can't cope with them. They are looting and burning palaces and killing whoever they choose. There is no way we can help Sir Baldwin.'

'We can't just leave him to die!' protested Alys.

'I'm afraid we must, mistress,' said Master Arkwright. 'I've no authority from your father to risk any lives of members of this household: indeed, we must save our strength in case our own house is attacked.'

Alys nodded, pretending agreement, but in secret she went off to the kitchen and asked for some old clothes. There was usually a bag of these near the outer door, kept to give out to deserving beggars when they came on their rounds. The news of the rebel assaults on London was all over the house, and the kitchen people huddled in corners frightening each other with stories and considering which of the kitchen knives would make good weapons. Alys said something about a dressing-up game and helped herself, unheeded, to the things she wanted from the bag.

In the hottest part of the afternoon, when the rebels there were drowsy after the share-out of what food they had been able to loot from shops in Cooks' Row, Alys arrived back at St Martin's church carrying a covered basket. The most wakeful of the villeins seemed to be the man who had so enjoyed the story about the bear, and Alys gave him a brilliant smile.

'Would you believe, friend, that my grandmother's asleep in that church — but I do think she must be!' she said with a giggle.

'I thought your grandmother was with the faithful departed,' said the man.

'No, no — that was the other grandmother — my foster-grandmother,' said Alys. 'We haven't seen this one since this morning. Do you mind if I go in and look? Another five minutes?'

'No more, then,' said the man, and he and several wakeful neighbours watched Alys as she walked unhurriedly back inside the church.

Sir Baldwin St George was still lurking behind the statue, but he had slid down to a sitting position. He scrambled up when he saw Alys.

'Well?' he said. 'Are they coming? How many?'

'They aren't to be had, Sir Baldwin,' said Alys. 'The city's in an uproar, with rebels everywhere. Nothing seems to be organized, and my father's not at home. You must take a chance, and just walk out with me: I've brought you a disguise. Be quick.'

She pulled out of her basket a huge and dirty blue dress, that had once belonged to the Ship House second kitchen-maid, a cloak and a dark grey hood.

'No, by the saints, that's too much!' said Sir Baldwin. 'Do you think I'm going to walk through London in broad daylight got up like that!'

'I think that if you don't, the rebels will get you,' said Alys, out of all patience with him. 'You can either stay or go. I'm going.'

'Wait then, wait,' said Sir Baldwin. 'And if you don't mind, look the other way.'

Somehow he struggled into the blue dress, and when he had covered it with the cloak and pulled the hood like a

Balaclava helmet down to his eyebrows and up to his chin, the result was not at all bad. Alys smothered a half-frightened giggle.

'It's good, but take your boots off,' she said. 'The spurs will show.' She remembered the man-woman, Long Lankin, who had so terrified her on the Hatley Road.

'What, and go in my stockings!' said Sir Baldwin.

'No — barefoot,' said Alys. 'You're poor now.'

Most of Sir Baldwin's clothes she stuffed into her basket and covered again with its rush lid; but the boots had to be abandoned. They were left, leaning against each other in a lopsided manner, behind St Martin's statue.

'Now, say your prayers, child,' said Sir Baldwin. 'And by the way, who am I?'

'My grandmother,' said Alys. 'We'll call you Pernel. Pernel Spicer. How's that?'

'Ghastly,' said Sir Baldwin. 'What do you think of my limp?'

All Alys said in reply was 'Sh' — they had reached the heavy church door. She pushed it open a fraction, and peered out.

They were in luck. Only the same few rebels seemed to be properly awake, and between these a fight had broken out. The bear-lover was the only one who really looked at Alys.

'Thank God, master, I found her safe and sound,' said Alys. 'Hours she must have slept!'

The peasant gawped at Sir Baldwin. 'What a fright,' he said. 'Lord, what a nose! I'm glad I don't have to live with her.'

'She's a dear old soul, really,' said Alys. 'Stone deaf, though.'

'Eh?' asked Sir Baldwin, in a wavering falsetto.

'Come along, now, granny,' Alys bellowed at him. 'We'll soon have you home.'

Sir Baldwin leaned heavily on her shoulder: his limp was not put on any longer, as his bare feet found the cobblestones an agonizing walk. Alys wound an arm round his waist, and the effort of balancing her basket as well kept her mind very well off the danger of the situation.

The next hazard was Mitchell, who refused point blank to allow a dirty beggar-woman in through the front door.

'Don't be an idiot, Mitchell!' hissed Alys fiercely. 'If you don't let us in, and fast, you'll lose your job as soon as my father gets home. I can explain — when we're in.'

'You'd best attend to the young lady, my man,' said Sir Baldwin in his own voice, pulling down his hood to show his face. 'Never heard of Sir Baldwin St George, have you — the bad baron of the Hatleys? Your master's landlord? Let us in quick.'

'Good God, Sir Baldwin — I know you by the nose!' gasped Mitchell. 'Come in at once, good sir.'

'And bar the door well behind us, Mitchell,' said Alys. 'Just a minute, though. You take Sir Baldwin to Master Arkwright; I want a quick look in the street. Just to make sure there's no one after us.'

Alys's quick look showed her that there were in fact a few rebels in the street, but they did not appear to be the men from St Martin's church. They were even dirtier and more ragged than those, and leading them at a rapid shamble was a man she recognized at once. Jack Carter from East Hatley, who had put her down in the road.

Alys forgot that this was a dangerous rebel, she forgot the unbarred door behind her. She shot towards Jack Carter with all her Castell fury up, yelling at him like a Viking warrior, 'Jack Carter! Jack! Just you wait — let me get to you — you stole my fare!'

Jack stopped dead, turned about, and was off like a hare in the other direction. To run from trouble was an instinct with him: and he could have been hanged for the theft of Alys's fare. 'Mad! Mad!' he screeched at the people with him; and perhaps Alys did look mad — scarlet-faced and stretching out a clutching hand to try to catch him, and howling blue murder. To a man, they turned tail and were off after Jack.

Alys returned, cooling as she went, to meet the startled stares of Mitchell, Sir Baldwin, and Master Arkwright. 'In heaven's name, Mistress Alys,' said Sir Baldwin, 'what did you say to them?'

'I knew one of them,' said Alys. 'He's a thief. I went after him, and they all ran.'

'Never met a girl like her,' said Sir Baldwin, and roared with laughter. 'Now then, masters, where can I change? And then I must greet the Lady Annis.'

'But suppose the rebels come back?' said Master Arkwright. 'Look to the north — there's a glare in the sky. If they're firing houses, our thatch may go up.'

Sir Baldwin was in his element. 'Get some of the apprentices up on the roof,' he said. 'Ladders, buckets. Give the thatch a good soaking; then if any stray sparks come this way they may not catch. Not too much, tell the lads: we don't want Lady Annis's house flooded.'

'Fill all the wash-tubs with water,' said Alys, entering into the spirit of siege. 'Then we'll have a supply of water handy if a fire does start. I'll get Edward: he'll love it.'

Annis Castell hurried downstairs, shortly, to find an amazing commotion. Mitchell, sweating like a horse, was winching up water from the courtyard well; Alys and Edward, wet to their eyebrows, were tipping it into tubs and buckets; half the apprentices were carrying buckets and the other half were on the roof; and operations were being directed by an outlandish old woman with her skirt hitched up to an unrespectable level. Lady Annis was not helped in her confusion when the old woman kissed her hand and asked after her husband, in a rich bass.

Edward said it had been the most exciting day of his life; but it had a long, tame interlude while they all waited for the rebels and the rebels never came. In the end they ate a picnic supper, Alys and Sir Baldwin properly dressed again, and Sir Baldwin proposed Alys's health in Sir Philip's best wine. 'And here's to the youngest Mistress Castell,' he said, 'who fetched me single-handed out of my captivity and who then frightened away a whole mob of peasants by shaking her fist at them. What a wife for a soldier! By heaven, Alys, I've half a mind to ask for you myself: I'm a widower now, and I need a new helpmeet.'

Alys blushed, looked at the tablecloth, and said nothing. She most sincerely hoped he didn't mean it. She guessed he was over sixty, and he was a long way from anyone's Sir Herriot Hendy.

Sir Philip's return home was so quiet that they didn't know he was in the house until he joined them in the hall. He crowned the joy of Edward's day by telling them that he had a boat waiting for them at the end of the lane: they were all to take refuge on his ship, *Marie*, until the rebellion was over and their house safe again. He patted Alys's shoulder when he heard how she had rescued Sir Baldwin, and called her his good daughter — but immediately added a sigh over her wild behaviour.

'She's revolting, like the villeins,' said Edward, who had got a bit above himself with the excitement of the day.

'Well, and if I am?' said Alys. 'Are the villeins altogether wrong, sir, when they can't get enough to eat, and their masters eat meat twice a day?'

'Don't be foolish, Alys,' said her father. 'The villeins are meant to be villeins: if they were meant to be gentlemen they would have been born gentlemen. It's all as God ordains. They rebel against God when they rebel against their masters.'

'This poverty — it's all invention,' said Sir Baldwin. 'They're as fat as pigs. They live well enough if they work for it. Some won't work, and that's the fact. Jack Carter who stole your fare to London — he's the type of troublesome devil who gets this sort of business up.'

Alys sighed. Jack Carter was certainly not a good

example of the deserving poor; but she thought of Emm and Sampson and their hard lives, and wondered if there was revolt in Harlton.

It was several days before the family, and Sir Baldwin with them, returned to Swan Lane. The house had remained undamaged: they were lucky. Other parts of London had had burning and pillaging and the stories of the rich being dragged outside and killed in the streets were only too true. Many of the Flemish community had been killed by the mob, whose hatred of foreigners had become confused with their grudge against the rich and the lawyers: anyone who couldn't say 'bread and cheese' was likely to be beheaded in the nearest gutter. Alys wondered, again and again, why there had been no second attack on Swan Lane, and what the guards around St Martin's had done when they finally went in for Sir Baldwin and found only his boots.

Alys's enterprise in going to Sir Baldwin's rescue was soon forgotten in the general admiration for a much braver thing: the young king had ridden out to confront the rebels, a slight, fair, fourteen-year-old facing a volatile rabble, and had made them promises of better treatment which had appeased them and put an end to the assassinations and destruction: promises which were not to be kept — but did he know that when he made them? Alys often wondered, but there was no point in asking questions. All the adults Alys talked to were too shocked at the violence of the Revolt to consider that the villeins had good reason for their discontent. 'The world is like that, Alys,' said her mother patiently. 'Now don't go on about it — it's a bore. Fetch me my scissors.' The only person who understood Alys's concern was Mitchell, who had been born a villein and who could remember his mother's struggle to feed a family of eight on bread and vegetables — many of the vegetables wild stuff out of the hedges and off the banks of the dykes.

'It's not my place to comment, Mistress Alys,' he said

to her. 'But if I still had rags on my back and scraps in my belly, I'd be slow to believe that it was God's doing and not that of the rich.' He told her too that even in her happy Harlton there had been trouble, and William Bateman's house burned down.

'Why him?' Alys asked. 'I didn't know that his people were overworked, or starved.'

'He's a justice of the peace, that's why,' said Mitchell. 'Standing for the law. They hate the law.'

Alys thought of Jordan, and then with less pleasure of Robert Fox. Would either of those law-clerks have been in a place of danger? Many lawyers had indeed been killed, and the Inns of Court where they worked set on fire; but a letter from Robert, saying that he was safe and listing his dead colleagues, soon set those particular fears at rest.

After such events, the rest of the summer was likely to be quiet. Sir Baldwin stayed a few days, worrying Alys by his elaborate compliments and all the attentions he paid her. She was glad when he went back to Hatley. After that there were parties and river-trips, and processions of Guilds and of clergy. Even so Alys drooped in the heat of London, and there was no chance of getting to East Hatley even when the countryside was cleared of rebels by a terrible revenge of hangings and fines. Lady Annis declared she could not face a journey, even the familiar one to her country home, and Sir Philip was pleased enough to be left in his counting-house. Edward fretted most — he was longing for riding, and to go out with the hawking parties.

Things were no better after Lady Annis's baby was born: for here another sorrow came to the house. The baby, a little girl quickly baptized Constance, died within a week of a wheezing cough which no medicine would help; and Annis herself was very ill, with a high fever which lasted for several weeks. All the girls helped to nurse her, and Christina returned to her old bed to take her turn. A doctor, Master Chillingfold, came and went, said a lot and did nothing, and at last Annis began to recover, to sit up in bed, eat a little fruit and drink Alys's mixtures of feverfew and vervain. During her convalescence Annis wanted Alys by her side constantly, to talk to her and sing; and Alys found herself growing in her father's favour as she worked herself voiceless to try to keep her mother entertained and cheerful.

'You are a dutiful daughter to us, Alys,' he said one day. 'I've had cause in the past to complain of you, but the way you have helped in nursing your mother has wiped that out. You are a true Castell, and none the worse for being brought up away from home. As soon as your mother is fit I shall take you all on some visits, to cheer up this whole house: we've never been ourselves since Humfrey died. In the meantime, is there anything you want for yourself — a pastime, perhaps, that I can arrange?'

Alys curtsied. 'Would you permit me, sir, to write a letter to Mistress Butler; and would you send it?' she asked, at her most polite. 'I should like to let her know that I'm well.'

'By all means,' said Sir Philip. 'Mitchell can go to East Hatley with it: I've other messages for him there. One of the Hatley people can ride across to Lordship Butlers.'

Alys got paper and pen, and — much hindered by Edward, who wanted to write a letter too — she wrote to Ede Butler:

> 'Honoured foster-mother, I greet you and desire you to know that I do well here and am grown tall and learn the French language. My sister Christina is wedded and, I suppose, Sisely too. My mother Lady Annis was brought to bed of a daughter but the child did not live, whereat we were all grieved and Lady Annis very sick. My brother Edward wishes me to send his greetings; he is six years of age and when he reaches seven years he will go to our uncle in Essex as a page —'

'No I won't,' said Edward, reading round her elbow.
'You may say you have my leave to write, and that I'll allow you to receive letters in return,' said Sir Philip, coming into the room with pompous good intentions.
'Oh, thank you, father,' said Alys, so overcome with pleasure that she forgot her manners.
Not only did Mitchell carry Alys's letter to Hatley, but he brought one back from Ede Butler. Sisely was married; Jordan had spent some time in Oxenford but had returned to his law studies in London, and so escaped the danger of being labelled Lollard, heretic, like many of those who listened to the teaching of Master Wycliff of Balliol; Maudlin Paunton was gone as a pupil to the nuns at Chatteris. The apple-trees were bearing well but there had been a poor crop of plums. All the family were in good health, and wished to send good wishes to her honoured parents and prayers for herself.
Alys read this unremarkable letter over and over, and passed the good wishes promptly to Sir Philip — who nodded, unsmiling — and Lady Annis, who looked vaguely pleased.
Before the winter weather set in, one more letter came for Alys — it arrived in time for her eleventh birthday, and slightly shamed the Castells who had forgotten the birthday altogether. This time Ede sent good wishes to all the girls as well, and Edward, and left them all wondering what she was like. But Alys couldn't reply. By late November there had been snow and heavy rain; the roads were so boggy that Mitchell wasn't sent to Hatley for poultry and firewood, and Alys couldn't send her Christmas messages for Ede and Hugh.
Christmas in Ship House, in spite of the presence of Robert Fox (Harry couldn't get himself a holiday), was quiet and decorous. The family went to midnight Mass, and there was a certain amount of games-playing with the clerks and servants of the household; but no Blind Man's Buff or Turn the Trencher, no forfeits and kisses. Alys's best Christmas present was a whisper from Christina, in a

dark corner, that the prayed-for baby would be born next June. Annora's best present was the announcement of her betrothal to a really rather agreeable man, not much above thirty, who was a client of her father's. Alys thought him wet and weedy, and his manners affected, but Annora viewed him with obvious relief.

'Not a patch on Sir Evremond,' Alys teased her.

'Oh, I don't know,' said Annora. 'He'd look nice in a tabard, on a destrier. He's got a very aristocratic nose.'

Alys gave up, and teased Jossey instead. 'You next,' she said.

'As long as it's Sir Herriot,' said Jossey; but she sighed.

Spring came late, and it wasn't until the end of April that warm days and good travelling weather led Lady Annis to remind her husband of his promise.

'Good Sir Philip,' she said, 'we were to go on some visits, weren't we? There'll be a fair at Smithfield, and perhaps a tournament. The girls will like that.'

'Me too!' shouted Edward.

'I had not forgotten, wife,' said Sir Philip. 'But first we shall all go down to Greenwich to see my new ship, *La Maudelayne*. We'll go down by river, and dine on the ship. Master Passmoor shall come.'

'In that case, I shall need a new dress,' said Annora: Piers Passmoor was her future husband.

'Get all the clothes made in good time,' said Sir Philip. 'In June we'll go down to Hatley, and you womenfolk and Edward will be spending the summer there.'

Alys was too old to jump up and down like Edward, but she couldn't restrain a skip or two. Hatley, in June — and it was already nearly May.

But the trip to Greenwich, and many other outings, were never to happen. In the middle of May Sir Philip came home early one day from a business trip, and came urgently into the solar where Annis and the girls were stitching in a pool of golden light.

'There's bad news,' he said abruptly, fanning his

flushed face with Lady Annis's fan. 'We must rethink all our plans at once, Annis. The pest is in England again, and the talk is that it's already in the city.'

The pest! Alys's mind shot back to Harlton, and the little children playing the game that acted out the red rash, the violent sneezing, the sudden death. The first outbreak of plague had killed huge numbers of people — some chroniclers said about a third of the population of England had died. Some farms had been left with no one alive to run them; some inheritances had gone begging because the second generation, who should have inherited, lay dead with their parents; and that terrible outbreak, called the Great Pestilence, hadn't been the end of it: there had been another three — less virulent, but still deadly. The last had been seven years ago, when Thomas Butler and the two Castell boys had died.

'Again!' said Lady Annis, clutching the wooden arms of her chair and staring with horrified eyes. 'I hoped to God we had seen the last of it. And oh, Sir Philip — Edward!'

Alys knew she was thinking of those three deaths, in that very house.

'Now we mustn't over-dramatize,' said Sir Philip (but why had he rushed home all in a sweat if the matter wasn't dramatic, Alys wondered). 'It may never reach this part of London.'

'We must leave,' said Lady Annis. 'We must leave at once. Edward especially. We must go to Hatley.'

'Now be reasonable, wife,' said Sir Philip. 'We must certainly go to Hatley. We'll send Mitchell to warn the Cheesemans we're coming, and he'll bring back the cart to take our luggage. It will take us a day or two to pack up clothes and plate; when Mitchell gets back we shall be ready to go.'

'But Sir Philip — Edward!' said Lady Annis. 'Edward must go at once. How can I sleep sound if Edward is here for a single day, half a day, in a plague-infested city!'

'I could go with Mitchell,' Edward offered eagerly. 'I could ride.' He saw his way to getting his own pony rather earlier than expected.

'You're not going anywhere alone with Mitchell,' said Sir Philip with decision. 'Granted he's no fool, Annis — six years old is still six years old.'

'Well, then — send someone else as well. But he must go,' said Annis.

'Nurse could go with him, or one of the serving women,' said Sir Philip.

'Oh, no, no,' Lady Annis protested. 'That would slow the journey down so! It would mean baggage, and a carriage, and a slower start —'

'Alys can come with me, then,' said Edward. 'She's always going on journeys. You will, won't you, Lys?'

'Be quiet, Edward — speak when you're spoken to,' said Sir Philip. Alys had the gumption to say nothing, but her breath came short. Was she going to see the Butlers again, and so soon?

'But what he says is sensible,' insisted Lady Annis. 'Alys wouldn't be afraid to go, and she would be a comfort to Edward. If they started now they could stop a night at an inn.'

'No inns,' said Sir Philip. 'The plague may be anywhere. Now if they started at first light tomorrow they could be at Osbern's by nightfall, and with a change of horses, at East Hatley by the following night. It would mean some fast riding, but the roads are dry. I had it in mind to tell Mitchell to ride at speed.'

'Can Alys ride that fast?' asked Annora.

Sir Philip looked at Alys, and she answered promptly. 'I'm out of practice, but I used to gallop a lot with the Butler boys,' she said.

'Alys will always do what she has to do,' said Jossey. Alys had no idea what she meant.

'Can they really not leave earlier?' said Lady Annis.

'No,' said Sir Philip. 'Not without staying in inns, which I don't intend they should. You'll have things to plan for them, wife: their clothes, and food to take in the saddle-bags.'

Both parents bustled away, and Alys and Edward danced a whirling dance of excitement round the room, holding each other's elbows.

'You're not so very special,' said Jossey. 'We shall all be in Hatley within a week.'

Yes, thought Alys, but by then I may have fitted in a surreptitious visit to Lordship Butlers. Her imagination expanded wildly. Suppose she could contrive a meeting between Butlers and Castells; suppose she could be a real Peace Child . . .

'What will you wear, Alys?' said Annora. 'Come on: I'll help you sort your clothes.'

'I wish everyone was going,' said Alys, remembering that other people had different preoccupations from her own. 'I wish we could take your Piers; and Christina, and the dogs.'

Although Alys had no nerves about the journey, she found it tiring and uncomfortable to a horrible extent. In order to give the chance of an exchange of horses during the day, Alys was mounted on a long-legged bay very much too big for her; Edward was perched up in front of Mitchell on a dark grey; and both horses carried saddle-bags. Alys was used to a rounder short-stepping pony, and found the long stride of her mount jarring and the effort to hold its head up a drag on her arms and shoulders. But she said nothing, and followed Mitchell at whatever pace he set.

They stopped at midday and rested the horses, and ate a meal sitting on a dry bank among the lush cow-parsley, with a rose-brier smelling sweet behind them. And after this they changed horses, to give the grey the lighter load. Perhaps the grey was already a little tired; at all events Alys found him easier to manage. She also got her dress more comfortably arranged, so that the skirts padded her knees and gave her some cushion between them and the saddle.

They got to Lord Osbern's house in the early dusk, and Alys was so stiff that when the same greasy-faced stable-boy lifted her down from the saddle she thanked him politely, and walked straight-kneed into the great house, hand-in-hand with Edward.

The welcome they had from their uncle was a warm and cheerful one. He scoffed at the idea of the plague: 'It will never get to Swan Lane,' he insisted. 'The little crowded houses will get it, where the people live like pigs in their sties. Your father need never have worried. But it brings me a visit from two little kinsmen, eh — and a chance to hear my minstrel niece sing, perhaps?'

Alys smiled faintly; but food, and a wash in hot water, eased her fatigue and she did sing. Not to the whole company, but to the ladies in the solar after dinner; where she also thanked her great-aunt Katherine for the money which paid her way to Lordship Butlers, and bought her her psaltery.

'We grieved and grieved about Humfrey,' said Lady Katherine. 'It makes Edward his mother's great treasure now, of course. No wonder if she's over-anxious for him.'

'He looks forward to coming to live with you,' said Alys. Edward opened his mouth to contradict, but Alys's quelling look kept him silent.

'And we to having him,' said Lord Osbern. 'Don't we, wife?' His wife, a very silent lady whose baptismal name Alys hadn't yet learned, nodded graciously; and Edward bowed his thanks — after Alys had given him a surreptitious pinch.

It was another early start next day. Lord Osbern had lent horses, so that the two from Swan Lane could rest. Mitchell was concerned about returning them, but Lord Osbern waved away his worry.

'When the whole family is settled in Hatley, they must all come visiting and return them then,' he said. 'It's no distance. This fuss about the pest will all die down in a couple of months, you mark my words. And it won't touch us here, of course; or come near Hatley.'

Alys felt cheered up by her buoyant uncle. She needed her good spirits, because the first half-hour after mounting again was awful — all of yesterday's aches came back with a vengeance. But riding itself eased them; and Alys enjoyed her uncle's horse — a lightweight but sturdy dapple-grey which she found easy to hold, in spite of its liveliness, and comfortable to sit.

'You're back in practice, Mistress Alys,' said Mitchell, whose mount was a fierce-looking black which went like the wind.

Alys didn't reply. She suspected the truth of the matter to be that her uncle's horses were a good deal better than her father's. Zephyr, the grey, carried her all day, as Mitchell's and Edward's charger seemed tireless.

'I begin to know these roads,' said Alys to Mitchell when they stopped to eat bread and cold chicken from Lord Osbern's pantry. The three of them sat resting on a fallen tree as they munched, and licked their fingers. 'We're not far now from the bridge and the hermit.'

'I remember the hut, but I've never seen the hermit,' said Edward. 'I wonder if she'll come out today.'

But there was no sign of her. 'She spies to see who's coming,' said Mitchell. 'A serving-man and two children wouldn't be likely to give her much; and she can't grab us as she grabbed you, Mistress Alys — she'd be afraid of a kick from a horse.'

'So much the better,' said Alys. Her preoccupation was getting to East Hatley, getting settled in, and making inquiries about her Butler family.

'Light's holding out well,' said Mitchell an hour or so later, as they paused to breathe the horses. 'We should be at the manor well before nightfall.'

'Light doesn't go faster or slower,' said Edward. 'You mean, we're going fast ourselves.'

Mitchell didn't reply, and Alys guessed that if Edward had been his little brother, instead of his master's son, Edward would have been thumped for being cheeky.

'Nearly there,' she said soothingly. 'Tired, Edward?'
'Hungry,' said Edward. 'I wonder if Mistress Cheeseman will have fish pie in the larder. Or venison pasty. Venison pasty would be good.'
'I only got soup, when I arrived late at night,' said Alys. 'But it was good soup. Hey, Edward, wait till I see that servant-girl who called me a little mistake. She'll call me Mistress Alys now.'
'So she will, or she'll lose her place,' said Edward.
Alys thought about this with satisfaction, as they rode on, and was adrift in day-dreams when Edward shouted, 'Mitchell, Alys — I can see a church; it's Hatley!'
'Thank goodness,' said Alys, as they slowed the horses to a walk up the sharp rise of Hatley Hill. 'It'll be wonderful to stretch, and walk about, and rest — Mitchell! What is it? Mitchell?'
They had reached the first two cottages of the village, and Mitchell had pulled the big black horse to a sudden stop. He stared, grey-faced in the dusk, at the door of the first cottage. It had, roughly chalked on the bare dark wood, a plain white cross. Alys reined in the grey.
'Look there, Mistress Alys!' said Mitchell, half whispering. 'Both doors — both houses — look!'
'But what is it? What does it mean?' Alys asked, her voice hushed too.
'It's the pest,' said Mitchell. 'That's the plague-sign on the doors. The pest's here before us, Mistress. It's in Hatley already. We can't stay here.'

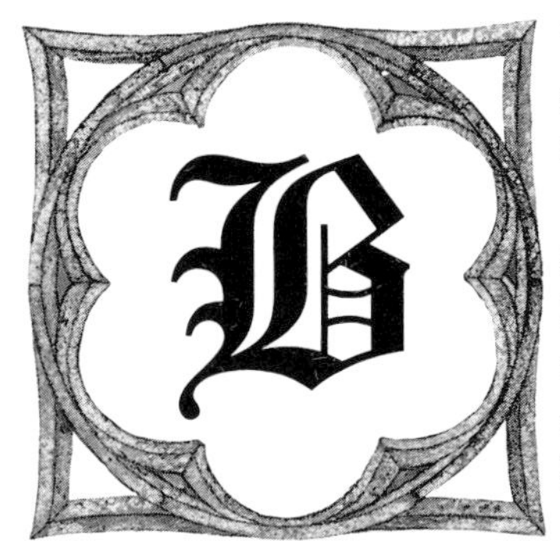

'But suppose the hall is safe?' said Alys. 'Suppose the Cheesemans are well, and —'

'I take no risks with you, especially not with Master Edward,' said Mitchell decisively. 'We came here to escape the pest; the pest is here. We must turn back.'

'But we can't, Mitchell!' exclaimed Alys. 'I'm tired half to death, and Edward's starving. It's clouding up for a dark night. We can't go back to our uncle's, as late as this.'

'We must,' said Mitchell. 'Your father forbade our having any truck with inns.'

Alys caught her breath. She knew what she wanted; what she had wanted all along. Did it take the pest to get it for her?

'We could go to Harlton,' she said. 'To Lordship Butlers. It's about six miles from here, across quiet country. We can be there before dark; and if there's no plague there, they'll take us in.'

'Oh, do let's, Mitchell!' urged Edward. 'I'd like to see the Black Butlers, more than anything.'

'But the Butlers —' said Mitchell, dithering.

'They're friends of my parents, now,' said Alys, hoping Heaven would forgive her exaggeration. 'They send kind messages back and forth by letter. You know.'

'But will they take you in — two Castell children?' said Mitchell.

'Try them!' said Alys, and laughed. 'They brought me up, Mitchell: do you think they'd shut the door on me?'

'They might, Mistress Alys, if they thought you brought the plague,' said Mitchell.

'Try them,' said Alys again. 'It's this way. And then we take the green road.'

They turned their horses' heads and rode for Harlton.

The Butlers were making all secure for the night, when the travellers arrived. Alys saw across the pasture, as they came from the Eversden side, the movement of Austin's lantern as he checked the doors of stable and byre, henhouse and pigsty.

'Hey, Austin!' she shouted across the moat. Austin's lantern bobbed as he straightened himself and peered towards them.

'Who's that,' he called, 'at this time of night?'

'It's me, Alys, and my brother,' Alys shouted back. 'Will you ask Master Butler if he'll come to the bridge and speak to us?'

It seemed only a moment before the door which led on to the bridge was unbarred, and Hugh Butler came striding across the bridge towards them. He had a lantern, too, but the darkness was not so far on that he needed any help to recognize Alys.

'Don't come any nearer, father,' shouted Alys, holding up a hand to stop his eager advance. 'Listen while I tell you. The pest is in London, though not at Swan Lane. The Castells sent me and Edward to Hatley, for safety; but we found the houses there plague-struck and we didn't dare stop. Will you give us lodging? We've stopped nowhere but at our uncle's house. But if you're afraid we may bring the plague, we'll ride away again.'

'What, in a starless night?' said Hugh Butler. 'And who rides with you, Alys?'

'Mitchell Harding, Sir Philip's man: your servant,' said Mitchell politely. 'We've ridden two days, or I'd turn back for London. I'm afraid we put you at risk.'

'No risk more than we take every day, in a plague year,' said Hugh Butler. 'All trade and meetings can't be stopped because of it, or all travel. We are in God's hands. Come along in, all of you. Daw, get this gate right open. Bring your lantern, Austin — here are two horses to be watered, rubbed down and fed.'

Alys slid off her horse into Hugh Butler's arms, and

kissed him warmly. 'And this is Edward,' she said, 'my little brother.'

Edward looked sulky.

'Well, you are,' said Alys. 'That's the one thing I didn't have, here. I had three big brothers, but no little ones.'

And then they were in the great hall, with old Kemp jumping at Alys, Ede sweeping her into a massive hug, and Ursel and Kate and Moll rushing for an immediate meal — which included duck patties, although there was no fish pie and venison pasty in the larder. Edward used his eyes and his teeth with energy, and Mitchell ate too at a side-table. Alys mainly used her tongue.

Finally, when dark had fully come, Alys yawned and asked for her bed. 'Can I share with Maud and Rose?' she asked. 'Is there room? I know I'm tall, but I'm not wide.'

'I want you with me, Alys,' said Edward, suddenly anxious.

'That will be best for tonight,' said Ede. 'You and Edward come into my and Master Butler's room, Alys, where we have the guest bed; after tonight we'll think again.'

'Oh, but, madam,' said Mitchell, standing up with a mug of ale still in his hand. 'Tomorrow we should ride back to Swan Lane. Sir Philip gave me no authority —'

'We'll talk of it,' said Sir Steven, polite but firm. 'With two bone-weary children, more than a night's rest may be needed.'

Alys said some fervent prayers that night: for the poor souls at East Hatley, struck down by the plague; for both her families, who must be allowed to escape it; and for herself and Edward, who must be left behind at Lordship Butlers when Mitchell rode back to Swan Lane next day.

Edward, quite unintentionally, settled it. He dragged himself out of bed next day complaining of an aching back and a sore seat.

'I know you like that black horse, Mitchell,' he grumbled, 'but its saddle *hurts*.'

'Poor lamb, he needs a day or two of rest,' said Ede Butler, all compassion. 'I do believe, Master Harding, you must ride back to London alone and leave the children here to recover. What can harm them here? Good country air, a simple life; no visitors calling to bring in the pest.'

Mitchell looked at the drooping Edward, and had to give in. 'I should take a letter back,' he said, still uneasy.

Sir Steven wrote it, and Mitchell rode off on the black horse, leaving the grey. Alys was delighted.

'When you're better, Edward, the grey will need exercise: I can ride it and you can ride my old pony — can't he, grandfather?' (She might call Ede and Hugh 'Mother Butler' and 'Father Butler', but Sir Steven was always 'grandfather'.)

'I see no reason why not,' said Sir Steven. 'Rose rides your Merry now, but she's a lazy rider and he hardly gets enough to do. Walter can take Master Castell hawking, if that would please him.'

Edward went pink to his ears. 'Well, I can't really ride,' he said; and Sir Steven gave him a benevolent smile.

'All the better,' he said. 'This is a good, safe place to learn. We have a quintain too, and all my grandsons ride at it.'

Edward's happiness was perfected. The quintain, a post and swinging dummy at which the boys rode with long sticks imitating lances, and pretended to be fighting in the lists, became at once his goal in life.

'When can I start?' he demanded. 'Tomorrow?'

'When you have a good firm seat at the canter, Master Castell, and not before,' said Sir Steven. 'Come with me now, and if you like I'll show you the sword I carried at Poitiers.'

'Edward's found a hero,' said Alys, contentedly going off to the dairy to churn for butter with Moll. 'I know what he'd like though, Moll; I must ask Mother Butler. He'd like to sleep in the tower.'

The small defensive tower had one room occasionally

used as a guest-room. It was draughty, and rather dark, being lit only by arrow-slits; and the spiral stair to it was steep. Alys was right that this was Edward's idea of a peach of a bedroom; and by that night it had been arranged that Alys, Edward and Ursel should sleep there. Edward still had a nurse, in London, and demanded Ursel — whose beacon of red hair caught his eye — to replace her.

'He doesn't still have a nurse, does he?' Ede Butler whispered to Alys.

'He does actually. She's old, and not much good with other work in the house, and Lady Annis doesn't want to turn her away,' said Alys. 'He can manage well enough without, though — he can do his own bows and buttons.'

'It'll do no harm, and Ursel seems to have taken a fancy to him,' said Ede. Alys wondered if Ede was anxious not to be compared unfavourably with the Castells in the matter of servants.

'That's not the only fancy that's been taken,' said Alys. 'Look at Edward with grandfather!'

'He must have heard the story of Poitiers seventeen times, if he's heard it once,' said Ede, smiling.

'I'm going to sit by grandfather,' said Edward, before dinner. 'He showed me his bad leg, where the swordcut is; all down from his knee to his heel, horrid!'

'Edward, I don't think you should call him that — he's not your grandfather,' said Alys feebly.

'Why not — you do!' said Edward. 'I haven't got any Castell grandfathers, so I shall be like you and have a Butler one.'

There was no answer to that. Alys could only hope that Sir Philip would not be too vexed.

'Four days,' said Edward happily at dinner. 'It will take Mitchell two days to get to London, and two to get back with father's letter saying what we are to do. At least. So we've got four days here — well, three, now — and I shall start riding tomorrow.'

'Edward, you talk too much,' said Alys, trying to be firm, but she thought — three more days! One to see the Butlers at the Spinney, one to see Emm, one to see the Pauntons — and then if Mitchell still didn't come, a glory of days just being at Lordship Butlers, free amongst the pastures and streams, riding and running with Walter and Maud and Rose and Edward; and always with Ede to come home to.

The freedom was brief; for on the fifth day after the children's arrival, Sir William the Harlton priest came to Lordship Butlers with a serious face. Walter and Edward were out riding; but Alys, scattering fresh rushes on the hall floor with Maud and Rose, heard what he said and stopped where she stood, rushes in hand.

'The pest is in Eversden, my good Hugh,' he said. 'I've called some helpers together and blocked the road in to Harlton — both ends of the village. We must stop it coming here, that last few miles, if we any way can. If you want to make the manor safe, you must block the green road too. And take what thought you can for your own people.'

Hugh swore, briefly but effectively, and begged Sir William's pardon afterwards. 'There's only one thing I can do,' he said. 'Break up my bridge and prepare to stand siege. I've two children here of the Castells, as well as my own.'

'If food runs short in the village, a siege is what it will be,' said Sir William.

'Don't think I'd let my neighbours starve, while I've got grain in the barn,' said Hugh. 'If food stocks do get low, I'll share what I have with them all. But I'll have water between me and the rest of the world. I'll come to the village now, with you, Father, and talk to the reeve. Then I'll fetch the people from Butlers' Spinney over to join us here. What safety we have, they shall share.'

'Some say the pest will cross water,' said Sir William.

'My father and I think otherwise,' said Hugh. 'And

suppose it does come to the village, Sir William, what will you do yourself?'

'Help the sexton dig a grave big enough to take half the people of Harlton, and prepare to be first in it myself,' said Sir William. 'What's the life of a priest worth in a plague year?'

The two men crossed themselves and Hugh went for his horse; Sir William was on foot.

'Shall I fetch the boys in?' Alys asked Hugh Butler; and when he said yes she went to find Lord Osbern's grey, eager to be doing something.

Edward was resentful of being called in from his riding; but when he heard that the manor was to be prepared to stand a siege he was more than enthusiastic.

'Break up the bridge!' he exclaimed with joy. 'Can I help? Shall we burn the planks?'

'No,' said Nicholas, overhearing this. 'The planks will make a raft for us, in case one or two of us need to go to land.'

The bridge was not a drawbridge, so the only way to take it out of use was to remove it altogether. The piles were left in the bed of the moat, but all the boards were torn up, and Nicholas and Daw set about making a raft of them. In the middle of the destruction of the bridge, came Mitchell.

'Mitchell! Mitchell!' shrieked Edward from inside the moat. 'You can't come over! I'm the king of the castle, and —'

Alys pulled him away. 'The pest is in Eversden, Mitchell,' she called. 'Master Butler means to keep us safe. Did you bring a letter?'

'A message only, Mistress Alys,' Mitchell shouted back. 'There was no time for writing. Your father first planned that you should go to Lord Osbern, but the pest is in Barkway too. He asked me to beg your foster-parents to keep you — you and Master Edward.'

'Gladly,' said Hugh, who had come to stand beside

Alys. 'And you, Master Harding? What will you do?'

'Stay here,' said Mitchell. 'The roads are blocked by now — they were working on it as I came through. And though I could ride away by the fields, I have my master's orders to stay near his children, and to take him word whether they live or die.'

'Do you want to come across?' said Hugh. 'You may, if you're prepared to work.'

Mitchell shook his head. 'I've been in inns and alehouses, Master Butler,' he said. 'I pray I'm not bringing pest to the village; but I'll make sure I don't bring it to your house. I'll lodge elsewhere.'

'There's no inn in the village,' said Hugh. 'Where will you go?'

'I'll ask the good priest to house me,' said Mitchell. 'If the pest does come, he'll need help.'

'And if it does come, you'll have signed your own death-warrant,' said Hugh. 'You're either a very good man or a very brave one, Master Harding — or both.'

The two men saluted each other, and Alys called after Mitchell, as he mounted his horse again, 'What's happening in Swan Lane, Mitchell? Are they all right?'

'They're all well, Mistress Alys,' Mitchell shouted back. 'If the pest comes close, they can go to one of Sir Philip's ships at Greenwich. They'll be safe on the water.'

'So they will,' said Hugh Butler; and Alys went indoors comforted. Annora, Jossey, her parents, and perhaps Christina too, could ride out the plague on the good ship, *La Maudelayne*.

By nightfall, the bridge to Lordship Butlers was gone and the new raft was beached in a quiet part of the farmyard. The Butlers' Spinney family — Richard, Adam, both Joans and Pentecost — had moved in and been found bed-spaces. A few cows had been brought in from the pasture, to give the household milk for butter and cheese, and were standing puzzled in the winter byre evidently wanting to be back among the buttercups.

Hugh and Sir Steven had checked barns and store-rooms.

'We can sit it out for months if need be,' said Hugh confidently to Ede. 'And there's grain to spare for the village if they want it. Simon Goodhew will come every day and bring news.' Simon was the reeve, the head and spokesman of the farm labourers of the village.

'I don't like it,' said Ede. 'We haven't got a priest: there will be no Mass. And I don't like to be cut off from our neighbours as if we were different, in God's eyes, from them.'

'What we are cut off from is the pest,' said Hugh briefly.

The older people might not like the siege, but the younger children found it immensely exciting. Until a day or two had passed: when the confinement to home began to be irksome to them. Alys and Rose fretted to get out to visit Emm or the Pauntons; Edward wanted his quintain. Hugh Butler spoke sternly to them all.

'A visitation of the pest is a punishment for our sins,' he said. 'Stop your grumbling, now, and try to improve your lives and your behaviour. Anyone I hear grumbling, I shall beat; Castells as well as Butlers. Unless of course you want to die of the pest: if you do, please say so.'

'What happens?' said Edward. 'Do you just sneeze, and drop dead? Like in the game?'

'Some people do,' said Hugh. 'But you may have huge swellings in armpit and groin, with agonizing pain; your wits may go and you may die screaming.'

Even Edward was impressed. 'Give me a bow and arrows, Master Butler, and I'll shoot anyone who tries to cross the moat,' he said.

The moat was crossed, but it happened at night when Alys and Edward were deeply asleep.

One bright day Sampson Baxter, Ursel and Emm's elder brother, came to the edge of the moat and bellowed a wish to see Ursel. Sampson was a boatman, sailing the local waterways with cargoes for Swavesey or

Cantebridge docks. He was home between trips, as his master's work was affected by the outbreak of plague. He stood laughing on the bank, his red head shining in the sun.

'And how did you get into Harlton, brother, with the roads blocked?' asked Ursel, laughing too, and Sampson winked.

'Wasn't I born here?' he said. 'Don't I know every guard on every road block? Your master is making altogether too much fuss about a small outbreak. It isn't even as violent a form of the illness as we've seen in the past. Can't you sneak out, Ursel? Come home tonight. I've got drink in: there'll be a party.'

'You know I can't,' said Ursel, looking quickly round.

'Nobody's listening; and you're not a child,' said Sampson. 'Be on this spot at midnight.'

'I can't use the Butlers' raft — it's too heavy for me to handle,' protested Ursel.

'Other people have got rafts,' said Sampson, and winked again.

Ten days later, on another bright morning, Ursel drew Ede Butler aside.

'Mistress Butler, I must go,' she said hoarsely.

'Go where, Ursel?' asked Ede. 'Nobody can go.'

'Home to my mother,' said Ursel, stepping back as Ede moved towards her. 'Don't touch me, Mistress. I must go.'

'We can't spare you, Ursel,' said Ede. 'What is all this?'

For answer, Ursel pulled open her dress; and on her chest, disfiguring the white skin below her throat, was a dark red rash.

'Holy God!' whispered Ede. 'The mark, Ursel, the mark! The plague — and here!'

'They call it God's token,' said Ursel. 'The people who have the red marks, the roses — they will die.'

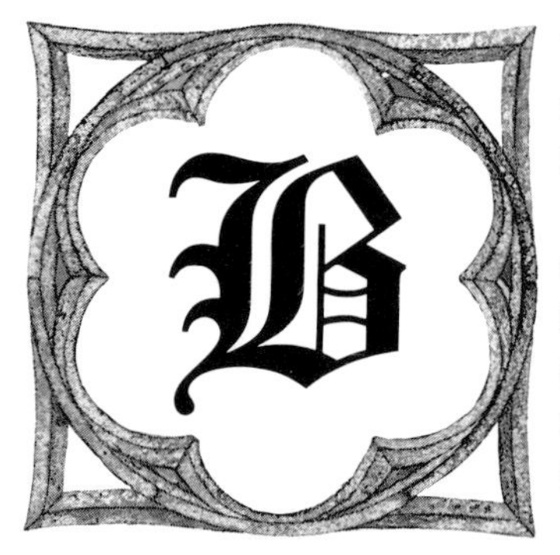

'But how could it happen?' asked Ede. 'When you've never left the farm?'

Ursel looked at the ground and spoke low. 'I did leave,' she said. 'Sampson is home; and he and Batt came at night, with a little boat, to take me to his party.'

'Then he brought the pest here, and may God forgive him,' said Ede. 'The village was clean before.'

'How could he?' said Ursel. 'He kept away from people and houses on his way home: he slept in a barn, to make sure.'

'How can we tell?' said Ede. 'Perhaps it lurks in barns.'

Ursel shook her head; but neither she nor Ede, nor the clever men like Dr Chiddingfold, knew that the busy scavenging rats who scurried from house to barn carried plague; and that the ravenous fleas who hopped from rat to human, and might live betweenwhiles in clothes or sacks or straw, took it further on.

'I must go,' repeated Ursel. 'I must see my mother before I die.'

'But suppose your family aren't ill,' said Ede. 'How can you go to the cottage, carrying death?'

'I shall stand outside and call,' said Ursel. 'If any of them are still untouched, I'll stay outside. I'll die in the churchyard, or in the street. I can't stay here, mistress — the children!'

'No, you can't stay,' said Ede. 'I'll call for Nicholas; he can float the raft for you.'

So Ursel crossed to the far side of the moat, and the raft and discarded paddle were pulled back at the end of a rope. Ursel never looked back, but stumbled away along the field path; and only Ede and Nicholas saw her go.

Ede, Nicholas and Hugh went to Sir Steven and talked over this calamity.

'Days she has had the illness on her,' said Ede. 'What chance have the children got, Alys and the boy?'

'God forbid they should die in this house,' groaned Sir Steven. 'Some hope of peace with the Castells then!'

'God forbid they should die anywhere,' said Hugh. 'But if they must die, let's save as many of the rest as we can.'

'You talk as if the two children were doomed,' said Nicholas. 'For all we know, they mayn't even be ill.'

Into the middle of this conference came Alys, innocently saying, 'Mother Butler, Edward feels shivery and his head aches. I've put him to bed. But where's Ursel — he wants her?'

The four Butlers crossed themselves, and Alys stared at them blankly. 'But what is it?' she said. 'He's only got a headache.'

'May God save us all, child,' said Sir Steven. 'It's to be feared he's got the plague.'

There was no time to be lost, and the Butlers put their practical minds to dealing with the disaster. Hugh refused to let Ede nurse Edward: 'No, my dear wife,' he said. 'I know you would do it but you have children of your own still young, and all this house to run.'

'He can't suffer all alone,' protested Ede, 'and Alys is not to be with him; she may not have the infection.'

Jillot, one of the farm girls, solved this dilemma.

'I'll be with the child, Mistress Butler,' she said. 'I've had the pest, seven years ago, and lived. Some say you never get it twice. And if you do — I've already been with Ursel.'

So Jillot went up to the tower bedroom to soothe Edward and sing to his headache; Alys, obeying the adults but desperately miserable, hung about the bottom of the tower. A bed had been made up for her in a clean corner of the hayloft above the stable, as she was the first to see that she should eat and sleep away from the rest of the family.

Ede Butler's sickroom preparations included burning Ursel's mattress and bed-sheet, and Alys's old bed too. Although the way the pest spread was a baffling mystery, Ede's private belief was that clothes and bedding could carry infection. In this she was wiser than she knew: they could carry fleas.

By the evening, Jillot reported that Edward was very ill: burning hot, suffering from painful swellings in armpit and groin. He couldn't eat the food which was sent up to the tower, and his only relief from his wretchedness was in sleep. 'There's no more doubt,' said Jillot. 'The poor little lad has the pest, and may God and St Gregory and the holy angels save his life.'

'We shall pray for him,' said Ede, handing Jillot the bucket of water for which she had come down.

'We'd best not meet again, Mistress,' said Jillot. 'Leave us food and water at the foot of the tower, and I'll bring the slops and the empty dishes down. I'll hang a sheet from the window if the child dies.'

Alys lay awake for hours on her solitary bed, praying, planning how the news of Edward's death could be broken to Lady Annis, and reliving her happy games with him. Twice she went down in the still moonlit night and looked up at the tower: there was no sheet in the window, yet.

In the morning, Edward was worse: delirious, and screaming. Alys stood at the foot of the tower and heard the thin, childish voice — not Edward's usual sturdy bellow — crying again and again, 'Alys! Alys!'

She went to the house-door and waited until Ede came out.

'What is it, Alys?' asked Ede, strained and grey-faced. 'Do you feel ill?'

'No — I'm all right,' said Alys. 'Mother Butler, I'm going to Edward. He screams for me, on and on. I'm going to go.'

'Not many people recover from the plague,' said Ede.

'Remember that, Alys. If you catch it from Edward, you are like to die.'

'I know that,' said Alys. 'He's my brother. I must go.'

'Hugh and I are responsible for you, to your parents,' said Ede. 'What will they say if they know I let you do this? If you die?'

'Tell them I disobeyed you,' said Alys. 'I make my own choices now, mother. I'm a Castell.'

'You always did,' said Ede. 'God's blessing go with you, and I pray you bring the child some ease.'

Alys went up the tower stairs at full speed, and sent Jillot away.

'Go down, Jillot, and save yourself,' she said. 'I'm nursing now. You can come with the food and water; I'll do everything else.'

'There's little use, Mistress Alys,' said Jillot. 'His wits are wandering. He won't know you're there.'

But Edward did know Alys. He clutched at her hand with his hot fierce grip, and the dreadful screaming died down. 'Stay, Alys,' he whispered. 'I have such horrible dreams. I dream I'm already dead and the rats are eating me. Oh Alys, Alys, am I going to die?'

'No, you're not,' said Alys. 'I know you're not, Edward, you haven't got the mark. God hasn't put his token on you. And there aren't any rats — not in a room of stone, like this. Here, I'll rest your head on my knee, and I'll tell you a story. Shall I tell you about Saint Gregory, who drove away the plague from Rome? He's the special saint of the English, because he sent the Word of God to us.'

'Yes, tell it,' said Edward, 'and say a prayer to him, Alys.'

So Alys sat, and held him; and although she could do little for the pain of the swellings, she soothed his anxieties and fears and kept him, for most of the time, hopeful and calm. He still sometimes had fits of delirium, but they seemed shorter now and less appalling.

On the third day Edward seemed better. One of the swellings had burst open, and was less painful; the others looked as if they might rupture too. He slept a lot; his bad dreams seemed to have gone and his skin felt cooler. Alys lay down to rest, and found she was too tired to get up again.

Nobody answered the door when Jillot came with food and water. Jillot toiled up the stairs and found Edward awake and alert and Alys in a heavy sleep, flushed and feverish and impossible to wake. She rushed back to the house and gasped out to Ede Butler.

'The boy looks like to live, Mistress — he's cooler, and his eyes are clear. But, oh dear, it's got our Alys.'

'We must pray,' said Ede, with a shake in her voice. 'They are robust children, well-cared-for and well-fed. If the boy can recover, Alys may too.'

Alys lost all count of days, and all difference between day and night. She was barely aware that Edward had been taken away, though she did understand when Jillot told her he was out of danger.

'Thank God,' whispered Alys. 'My mother would have died to lose him. Jillot, come here and look at my chest — have I got the marks?'

'No, nothing: white as a lily-flower,' said Jillot.

'That's my name,' said Alys, and lost herself again in a maze of phantoms and dreams.

When she next woke to her clear senses, after days had passed, it was to a feeling of coolness and air. The room was bright in a rosy sunset, and Ede Butler and Annis Castell were at the foot of her bed, both in tears and clasped in each other's arms. Alys thought it was a vision.

'Have I died?' she asked them. 'Is this paradise?'

Annis's tears turned to hiccups of laughter, and Ede patted her on the back.

'No, Alys dear,' Ede said. 'It's the old tower, and Lordship Butlers; same as ever.'

'Am I dying, then?' said Alys. 'Is that what you're crying for?'

'No, no,' said Annis. 'You're better, child; we're only happy.'

Alys looked at the two of them, and thought — though she had no energy to say it — 'I've still got too much to do, to die. I'm the Peace Child.'

Alys's recovery was draggingly slow. Edward bounced back to health in a few weeks, and was able to enjoy being the centre of attention and having his mother at Lordship Butlers on his account.

'I've had the pest, and lived,' he told everyone, full of his own importance.

'You should be ashamed,' Walter finally told him, flaring up, 'to brag about what was just your good luck. Twenty people in Harlton are dead, one of them your own Mitchell.'

This sobered Edward. He did grieve for Mitchell buried in the common grave with so many of those who had become his friends.

But Alys coughed and coughed, could eat little, and was a long time even in sitting up in bed. The news from the village didn't help her. Bright, talkative Emm was dead, lying in the churchyard with Ursel and Batt and dancing Sampson who had led the farandole — and led the plague to Harlton.

When the pest was reckoned to be gone from the village, the one survivor of the Baxters came creeping to Lordship Butlers and stood calling by the moat. Old Emma, really looking old now with her pale and withered face, shouted for Alys until Jillot came to her.

'It's no good your calling Mistress Alys, Emma,' she said shortly. 'She's still in her bed, and much too ill to come.'

'But she'll live?' said Emma.

'No thanks to you and yours,' said Jillot.

'Send me the mistress, then, Jillot,' begged Emma. 'Send me Mistress Butler.'

Ede Butler went. 'Well, Emma?' she said. 'What is it?'

'I'm the only one left, Mistress,' said Old Emma. 'My

beautiful girls are gone, and my proud boys. My neighbours are against me now, because they say our Sampson brought the plague. They've burned my little house and turned me away.'

Ede clicked her tongue. 'That was bad,' she said. 'You're not to blame for Sampson's doings.'

'They said the house was harbouring pest,' said Emma. 'Oh, Mistress Butler, let me come over, do. I've no roof and only the stubs of walls. I'll nurse your little Alys — I'm strong, and I've had the pest. She'd like to have me. And I'll bake for you, and wash clothes.'

Aunt Joan advised against it, but Hugh and Richard and Sir Steven left the matter to Ede. So Old Emma was towed across on the raft and given new clothes, her old ones burned on the rubbish heap; and she went to share Alys's tower room and wait on her, combing the tangles out of the long hair and amusing Alys with stories and rhymes and riddles. Emm's rhymes, Emm's riddles. It was like a pain in Alys's mind to hear them, but she would rather be reminded of Emm than forget her.

When Alys was no longer in any danger of dying, Lady Annis took Edward and went back to Lord Osbern's where Christina and Annora and Jossey were. Lord Osbern's manor had not been touched by the plague and Annis decided to sit it out there until either London or Hatley was felt to be safe. Sir Philip was on *La Maudelayne*, and Rayner Ballaster with him. Alys prayed her thankfulness, every day, that her own family were all saved, and the Butlers too; though she often cried for Emm.

'You shall come to your uncle's, Alys, as soon as you're really strong,' said Lady Annis as she rode away. Alys watched the horses over the bridge (back in place now, and as good as new) and sighed over her divided feelings.

'When my mother made me a Peace Child, she stopped me ever having any peace myself,' said Alys sadly to Ede that evening.

'Oh, be thankful, child, be thankful,' said Ede,

looking up from spinning. 'You have two families that love you.'

'I know, and I should be ashamed,' said Alys. 'Give me some work to do; that'll stop me grumbling.'

Life in the village slowly returned to something approaching normal. Parties were held; there was a great rush of christenings and a small rush of weddings. Annora was married, too: a letter came for Alys with a gift of gloves from Piers. Annora had been married from her uncle's house, and had gone back to London with her new husband. Christina was back in London too, with Thomas, her new little son. London was returning to normal even faster than Harlton. Alys was sorry to have missed Annora's wedding and Thomas's christening, but didn't wish herself anywhere other than Harlton.

After the harvest — gathered as well as possible with the reduced workforce — rain and stormy weather came. Alys thought of the autumn when she had first left Harlton, two years ago. Now, as then, there was a feeling of change coming; and she was not surprised when one morning Rose summoned her to Sir Steven's parlour.

'You guess why I want you, Alys,' he said.

'Yes,' said Alys. 'I can guess. My parents have sent for me.'

'Not yet,' said Sir Steven. 'But you and I both know they soon will. They will return to their London house, and want you with them, before the winter sets in.'

'Oh, grandfather,' sighed Alys. 'Are you sure they'll want me?'

'Ask yourself,' said Sir Steven. 'Are you?'

'Yes, I suppose so,' said Alys. 'Annora is married; and I expect my mother will leave Edward behind at my uncle Osbern's. He's just on seven now.'

'Yes,' said Sir Steven. 'You have good parents, Alys; they will make a good marriage for you, with a kind man.'

'I know,' said Alys. She thought of Sisely, who had come over when the plague ebbed to see the Butlers and exchange news. Sisely could not hide the dark bruises on cheek and arm; and all the family knew that the high-spirited Everett was a deal less kind than one might wish him to be. 'But oh, grandfather,' Alys added, 'I don't want to leave here. To leave Mistress Butler and all of you; and the farm.'

'Needs must, Alys,' said Sir Steven. 'You belong to your parents, not to us: that contract is over. If they send for you, we shall yield you up, no question. We want peace with them, not war. And I'm sure you'd prefer to return in comfort, not fetched by Robert Fox and Harry Brag.'

'I know,' said Alys. 'I certainly don't want any fighting over me — even a fighting in words. I know I've no choice.'

'One choice you do have,' said Sir Steven. 'Palatable or not. Nobody would stand in your way, I believe, either Butler or Castell, if you wanted to become a nun.'

'A nun!' said Alys, staggered at the thought. 'But I'm not twelve yet. You can't take vows till you're twelve.'

'True,' said Sir Steven. 'But you could go as a pupil, like Maudlin Paunton; with a view to becoming a nun in some years' time.'

'I don't think I'm good enough,' said Alys.

'Very likely not,' said Sir Steven in his driest voice. 'I've noticed you don't go in for meekness to any great extent. I'm not making suggestions, Alys; only pointing out you have a choice. Not between Butler and Castell, but between Castell and God.'

'It is a choice, I suppose,' said Alys slowly. 'If I chose to be a nun, I should be choosing peace.'

'I wondered about that,' said Sir Steven. 'So far the choices made for you have been about other people's peace, not your own.'

'Could I go and see? Go and visit Maudlin in the Benedictines' house, and see how they live?' asked Alys.

'No harm in that,' said Sir Steven.

The best way to Chatteris, in the middle of a wet autumn, was not by road at all but by water. Chatteris was on a fen island, and the road towards it from Cantebridge would by now be deep in mud; moreover the unrest of the previous year, and this year's plague, meant that there were many homeless men on the roads, and highway robbery was rife. The law couldn't keep up with all the burglary and banditry; and people in boats were much safer from attack than people on horseback or in carriages. Nicholas, Walter and Maud were given leave to go with Alys as an escort: they had been much cooped up all summer and Hugh and Ede thought they would all be better for a change of scene before the bad weather came. Rose cried blue murder at being left behind, but Ede said firmly that Rose was too young for the trip. Alys wondered whether Ede might be afraid of Rose's deciding to become a nun, too: she and Maudlin were much of an age and had once been close friends.

The four young people took Jillot and Daw to wait on them, and show that the Butlers were a family of good standing with servants to spare for expeditions. They all rode into Cantebridge, stabled their horses there and took to the river. Alys — and perhaps the others, too — thought of Sampson when a hefty young fellow called Sim agreed a price to take them all to Chatteris and settled them on board his barge; but she could not feel melancholy for long. The barge itself was interesting: a long, narrow boat with in its middle a space covered with a canvas hood, and with cushioned seats for passengers. Alys had seen boats like this before, but had never been on one. Sim and his mate, Sefrid, poled the boat along with long poles; they carried on board two spare poles in case of accidental loss of one that was in use, or the need to enlist more pole-power if they ran into difficult currents. Nicholas and Walter both hoped that this would happen and that they could take a hand with the boating.

At first, on the River Granta, they met quite a lot of

other traffic. They came alongside a barge like Sim's, but loaded with grain. It was going to the Abbey of Croyland with part of the crop from one of the Abbot's farms. The boatman was a friend of Sim's, and for a time the two boats ran side by side with cheerful and teasing shouts from one to the other. But Sim's load of people was lighter than his friend's heavy weight of corn, and finally the abbey boat was left behind.

It was a long, slow day for the Butlers, especially the girls. Nicholas and Walter did get their turn with a pole, for Sim and Sefrid were glad enough to rest, but Maud and Alys were only allowed to watch. As the Granta flowed into the long dyke that joined it to the Ouse, and on into the Ouse itself, one flat, dull stretch of fenland, with scrub and swamp and banks of willows, succeeded another. They did stop at an inn on the riverbank, for food and ale, and it was a relief to stretch and walk about after long sitting.

It was dusk when they got to Chatteris, and Sefrid guided them through the lanes to the nunnery. The falling darkness meant that they could not go to see the buildings of the nunnery that night. They did go to the service of compline in the church, which seemed to Alys a huge and draughty building in which the candles flickered and flared. She didn't see Maudlin; but nodded through the singing of the nuns and had to be propped up as they all went, drowsy, to the guest-house for the night.

The next day a smiling girl of about sixteen, called Aldrith, showed the four of them around the buildings. Alys thought the nunnery the most beautiful place she had ever seen — better even than Lord Osbern's great house, or some of the grand mansions she had seen in London. Stone-built, with a walled orchard and gardens, and tall windows of coloured glass in the church, it had grace and serenity which seemed to cry out to her that this was what she needed: this was security, an end to questioning, an end to the tide that washed her from

Butler to Castell and back again, a choice of her own at last.

The others left Alys in the nunnery and went off to see Chatteris. Alys sat on a bench in a cool, bright room and tried to compose her feelings. The Abbess herself would see her; and when she was ready, Aldrith came to fetch Alys and take her there. The Abbess, Dame Margery Hotot, had a small plain room of her own; and thrilled Alys by calling her Mistress Castell. She immediately afterwards disconcerted her, however, by asking after Sir Baldwin St George.

'Your neighbour at East Hatley, isn't he?' said Dame Margery. 'One of our benefactors: he gave us the glass for our church, you know.'

'I don't know him well,' said Alys. She was really quite cross to think that she couldn't escape from Sir Baldwin, even here. But at least nobody here would expect her to marry him.

'And what do you come to find here?' asked Dame Margery, her keen dark eyes — almost as black as a Butler eye — resting on Alys.

'Peace, I think,' said Alys.

'For yourself?' said the Abbess.

'Yes,' said Alys. 'Is that selfish?'

'Maybe,' said the Abbess. 'You have to decide, Mistress Castell, whether your own peace comes first, or the peace of the world.'

'If I lived here, I would pray for the peace of the world,' said Alys. 'That's what you do, isn't it?'

'Yes,' said the Abbess. 'And I don't deny it needs a soul at peace with itself to pray well. But be careful, Mistress Castell. Some who come here looking for peace find only the sword.'

'Do you mean, some people have unrest in their own minds?' asked Alys. 'So they can't find peace anywhere?'

'Indeed,' said the Abbess. 'And for those people, peace is better looked for outside a wall rather than inside it.'

'Some people have to do other things for peace, then, instead of praying for it,' said Alys.

'Certainly,' said the Abbess. 'Now go on your visit, dear child; walk around; see your friend Maudlin. Try to feel whether peace for you is an indoor matter or an outdoor matter. If you choose to come here, you will be welcome.'

Alys curtsied, and went off with Aldrith to look for Maudlin.

Maudlin was with a group of young girls, five of them, reading in a rather dark room. She leapt up when she saw Alys, flung her arms round her neck, and hung on to her, laughing and talking, unstoppable.

'You can walk out with your friend, Maudlin,' said Aldrith; and Maudlin led Alys, at a great pace, to the orchard and sat her on a bench under a loaded apple-tree.

'Now, tell me everything,' said Maudlin eagerly. 'All the village news. And my family. Is Eve married yet?'

'Don't they write?' asked Alys, and Maudlin's face clouded. 'No,' she said sadly. 'They don't, Alys; I think they've half forgotten me.'

'Do you miss them?' asked Alys.

'Not the way I did,' Maudlin confessed. 'I used to cry for them, all the time. Now it's only sometimes.'

'Wouldn't they take you back?' said Alys.

'No,' said Maudlin. 'How could I ask them? My father can't afford a dowry for me; he told me so.'

'But he'll pay a dowry to the nunnery, when you take your vows,' said Alys.

'Not so much; and no land,' said Maudlin. 'He won't part with land; and the nuns don't insist on that. I'm the fifth girl, Alys. He can't afford me. I can never go back. I suppose in time I'll forget them too.'

Alys looked at the round, ten-year-old face, with its straight hair and faint scatter of freckles, and was filled with sadness and compassion.

'Tell me about your life,' she said. 'Are the nuns kind to you? What do you do?'

'They're the kindest people in the world,' said Maudlin. 'They teach us girls; not just reading and Latin and things — we learn to sing, too. You'd like that, Alys. We learn to sing the services. We have to listen a long time first; but they've let me start to sing.'

'Yes, I'd like that,' said Alys. 'And what do you do besides?'

'We talk, and sew, and walk around at recreation times,' said Maudlin. 'We can play ball, or shuttlecock, if we're quiet about it. It's not so different from being at home. The beds are warm and there's enough to eat. We can't have pets, though. Luce used to have two little birds but she was told she shouldn't. She was upset.'

'But, Maudlin, don't you ever really play?' said Alys. 'Our old games — *Here comes three dukes a-riding*, and *Good ship sails*, and *Wallflowers*, and *Roman soldiers*? Don't you dance — the branle and the farandole? You're only girls, you five.'

'No,' whispered Maudlin, and tears rolled down her plump cheeks. 'The nuns would think it worldly, and they are so patient and good to us. Oh, Alys, what I wouldn't give — the farandole again, with you and Maud and Wat and everybody! The dances at Harlton, on the green, at harvest-time!'

Maudlin cried again, to say goodbye to Alys. 'And will you come back, Alys? Will you come to stay?' she asked eagerly. 'How I'd like to have you here, and talk about home!'

'I know, I know,' said Alys. 'I've got to think, Maudlin; I've got to decide.'

She said the same thing to the Butlers, who were waiting for her at the gate when she said goodbye to Aldrith there.

'What will you do, Alys? What will you do?' demanded Maud, frantic with impatience.

'I don't know,' insisted Alys. 'I've got to think.'

And that was all she would say as they made their way back to the wharf, and found Sim and Sefrid, and were punted home — all she would say to Ede and Hugh and Sir Steven when she got back to Lordship Butlers and was bombarded with offers of food and drink, and questions.

But the next person who asked her got a comprehensible reply.

In the early dusk she went walking to stretch her legs and ease her worries; and in Butlers' Spinney, where the gold-brown hawthorn leaves were beginning to drift into the hollows, she met Jordan leading a horse.

'I didn't know you were home, cousin,' she said. 'Why aren't you at your work in London?'

'I've work to do in Cantebridge: I just called home on my way,' said Jordan. 'Have you decided, Lilyflower?'

'Yes, I think so,' said Alys. 'I don't think I shall go, Jordan, and be a nun. I'm not good and holy: I want things too much, and I want to dance and play and sing our songs. The Abbess warned me that a nun's life didn't bring everybody peace.'

'You'll have to work your peace out in the world, then,' said Jordan. 'I'm glad, Alys; and so will all the Butlers be. Perhaps we need you — coming and going among the Butlers and the Castells.'

'No more coming and going, Jordan,' said Alys, with regret. 'I shall go back to the Castells, now, and I shall stay; and my father will marry me to a rich old man and oh, dear, how grim it will be.'

'Has he got someone in mind for you?' asked Jordan.

'He hasn't said,' said Alys. 'But Sir Baldwin St George said he liked me; and I don't like him, Jordan, not in the least.'

'I should think not!' said Jordan. 'He's an old rogue. There would be only one thing to be said for that — you could ride over to Harlton to visit us all, when you were at Hungry Hatley.'

'There's another good thing too,' said Alys. 'At least he's better than Robert Fox or Harry Brag.'

'True,' said Jordan. 'And them you can't be expected to marry, seeing they're your half-brothers. The law allows some funny things, but at least it won't allow that.'

Alys was back in Swan Lane before her twelfth birthday; and this time the Castells remembered it — especially Jossey. 'Oh, Alys,' she said as soon as Alys set foot in the house, 'you can't know how pleased I am to have you back. We were all so scared you would die. I've never said so many prayers — not since Humfrey, anyway. It's been so hideously quiet here, without you and Edward. And for a time father was very angry that you'd got the plague at the Butlers' — as if it was their fault. He calmed down when he knew Edward was getting better.'

'I'll change all that,' said Alys. 'We'll have some good times, Jossey. Remember Herriot Hendy?'

'Yes, I do,' said Jossey, and giggled. 'Lys, it seems as if I haven't laughed since you went away. I know you'll miss the Butlers, and it's hard; but maybe we'll get to Hatley in the Spring.'

'Third time lucky,' said Alys cheerfully, and went to kiss her mother's hand and take her kind greetings from the Butlers. Lady Annis kissed her forehead and said she was to have a silver ring for her birthday; Sir Philip was gracious and asked about her health.

'Not many men have two children survive the plague, Alys,' he said; and Alys realized with surprise that he was congratulating himself on the strong constitution he had passed on. Or in having in some way weakened the force of the disease.

'They said it wasn't as bad as the first outbreak of all,' she said unhelpfully. 'And that the people who fell ill later, as Edward and I did, had a better chance than the ones who caught it first. And we live clean and feed well here, and so do the Butlers. The poor people in crowded houses, living on scraps and not even enough bread — they couldn't fight it off.'

'Still,' said Sir Philip, not much deflated, 'we have a lot to thank God for.'

So you have, thought Alys — and to thank the Butlers for, too. She went to find out from Jossey where Harry Brag and Robert Fox were.

'They're in father's black books,' confided Jossey. 'They've both gone off. Harry left his post, and Robert's thrown up his study of the law. Harry took away a rich young woman from her family, and meant to make her marry him, and Robert helped; but her brothers came after her, six of them, and Harry and Robert had to leave her behind and run for it. They're hiding; we don't know where. Father's hot as fire against them, especially Robert — which isn't fair. He wanted a lawyer in the family.'

'To be honest, Joss, I'm glad they're away,' said Alys. 'I can't ever get over being captured by them.'

'It's always more comfortable without them,' Jossey agreed. 'They irritate our honoured father; and I'm not sure our honoured mother isn't afraid of them.'

Alys exulted privately, and put a message to Jordan at the end of her letter to Ede Butler. 'Harry and Robert are gone, nobody knows where; Sir Philip is not seeking for them,' she wrote; and hoped that the Butlers in general, and Jordan in particular — if he ever got this piece of news — would know how much easier this made her life in London.

Lady Annis now began an intensive campaign of drilling her two remaining daughters in manners and deportment, dancing and dress.

'They're working themselves up to marry us off,' said Jossey.

'Not me — not yet,' said Alys. 'I'm only twelve, Joss. You could be married this summer, if father put his mind to it.'

'Next summer, I expect,' said Jossey. 'I need time to practise dancing. I do wish I could dance like you; you're so natural.'

'I was brought up on it,' said Alys. 'I'm too boisterous, though; I like to fling about, and stamp.'

'It's your villein childhood,' said Jossey. 'No — stop — I'm only joking!' as Alys went for her. 'You know I'm jealous, really. I should have loved to dance the farandole through the cowpats.'

'I'll teach it to Sir Herriot,' said Alys.

But there was no sign of Sir Herriot; and Jossey began to wear the anxious look Alys had hated to see in Annora. 'How should I love, and I so young,' Alys sighed to herself over her embroidery frame.

She had her own worries. Sir Baldwin St George was back in London. He called on her father with letters and news from East Hatley, and stayed to dinner. He said nothing special to Alys, but he looked at her in a sharp and interested way and Alys became too agitated to finish her apple fritters. He came again just before Christmas, and Alys pretended to be ill and missed dinner altogether. It was worth it, and Jossey brought her a chicken leg smuggled in a napkin.

After that he must have gone back to Hungry Hatley: there were no more visits, and Alys was able to forget him again.

One day in April, when she was curling Jossey's hair in the bedroom, Sir Philip sent for her. He was alone in the solar, as Lady Annis was visiting Christina, having said she wanted Christina and Thomas to herself for a time.

Alys stood in front of her father and rapidly ran through all her current faults and failings. What was the reprimand to be for this time?

'Daughter,' said Sir Philip, 'the time has come when I want to talk of your marriage.'

Alys felt as if she had fallen from a tall horse down a steep cliff.

'Mine, sir?' she said, aghast. 'But Jossey is the elder: Jossey should be married first.'

'I'm not implying you will be married first,' said Sir Philip. 'It may be appropriate for you to have a long betrothal — two or three years, perhaps. Don't vex yourself about Jossey; I have plans for Jossey, but there are complicated arrangements to make.'

'Oh,' said Alys.

'There are reasons, Alys, why I should like your marriage fixed,' Sir Philip went on. 'You have had an unsettled life so far, with a lot of changes. To have things all in order, and your mind at rest, will be best for you; and other people to whom I owe thanks will be glad of it, too.'

Alys couldn't follow him.

'The advantage to me,' Sir Philip said, 'will be to marry you to a distinguished man, and a man who will be of assistance to me in my business.'

Alys felt her old fears surfacing. Could it really be Sir Baldwin he had in mind? He would certainly help her father's affairs — holding, as he did, the Hatleys in his hand.

'I had hopes of Robert there, of course,' Sir Philip went on, 'but Robert has failed me.'

'Is it a friend of Robert's?' asked Alys, dreadful new possibilities rising up before her. No friend of Robert's, she felt, could be anything other than hateful.

'An acquaintance,' said her father. 'Now understand me, Alys. I won't force this marriage on you if you have good reasons against it — if for any reason it repels you. If it does, you must tell me.'

Alys felt a kind of despair. How would she ever find the courage to tell her father she could not bear to marry Sir Baldwin? And surely it would make no real difference if she did; in spite of his kind words, her father expected obedience. She made him no answer except to curtsy deeply.

'Now go along and meet him,' said Sir Philip, suddenly smiling. 'He's in the parlour of my counting-house. Go on.'

'Oh — not on my own!' begged Alys. It struck her as most improper.

'I'm rather busy, your mother's out, and Jossey has one side of her head curly and the other straight — or had when she looked round the door just now,' said Sir Philip. 'Go on; then come and tell me how you like him.'

Alys went, trembling and sticky-handed, to the counting-house, and crept round the parlour door holding her breath. In spite of the remarks about acquaintances of Robert, it was still Sir Baldwin St George she expected to see.

With his back to the room, looking out into the street, was Jordan Butler.

'Oh — Jordan! It's only you!' exclaimed Alys in profound relief. 'You chose a good time to call: Harry and Robert are still missing. It's not like my father to tease, but he told me — he told me —' She faltered and Jordan came to her laughing and kissed her hand.

'Is it such an outrageous idea, Alys?' he said. 'Couldn't you contemplate marrying your cast-off cousin?'

'Is it true, then, Jordan?' whispered Alys. 'Marry you — I can think of nothing, nothing, I should like so much in the world.'

'That's lucky,' said Jordan. 'I rather fancy it, too.'

Alys hurled herself at him, and they clasped each other in a crushing Butler hug and danced a thumping Butler dance around the room. The parlour table went flying and Hubbard put a nervous head round the door. He removed it at once.

'How soon can we be married?' asked Alys, when they stopped for breath.

'Not for three years or so,' said Jordan. 'But we can enjoy ourselves now making plans.'

'I don't want to wait,' said Alys. 'And oh, Jordan, did

you ask for a huge dowry? Sir Philip can perfectly well afford it; and we shall need a house, and cutlery and table linen, and hangings for the beds, and you know twins run in the family.'

'An absolutely huge one, Lilyflower,' said Jordan. 'He'd pay to get rid of you.'

'And to think,' said Alys, hanging on Jordan's elbow, 'that I was wanting to marry Sir Herriot Hendy! What a mistake.'

'I'm sure it was,' said Jordan. 'Who's he?'

'We'll get married at Hatley, so all the Butlers can come,' said Alys. 'Sir Philip can dance with Ede, and Lady Annis with Hugh, and Nicholas with Jossey; and I'll dance with grandfather.'

'And who do I get?' complained Jordan.

'Lady Katherine,' said Alys. 'She'll fix you; she's terrifying. And Jordan, can we have Roger Hall and Hawkyn Harper to play at the wedding?'

'We'll have the lot of them,' said Jordan. 'Girls and all. Though I'm afraid it will shock Lady Katherine.'

'She wasn't shocked when I sang,' said Alys.

'Deaf?' asked Jordan; and Alys, delighted, dragged him off to meet Jossey. Who stared completely silent, her whole attitude plainly saying that Jordan — who had grown very tall, and was a curly-haired Butler with a sparkle in his eye — was better than Sir Herriot to her way of thinking, too.

Jordan's goodbye to Alys, after he had eaten dinner with the Castells and entertained Sir Philip with accounts of legal scandals, was a whisper behind the door.

'I forgot to say,' he said. 'My father will give us some land near home when we marry. I'm planning to build up my work in Cantebridge, Alys, and to live in Harlton one day.'

Alys stretched up and kissed his chin. 'Wasn't it a good thing I didn't become a nun?' she asked.

'You were right,' said Jordan. 'Your job is out in the

world. You and I, we'll settle the Butlers and the Castells, once and for all, and make them behave themselves properly — peaceable and mild.'

'What, even Harry Brag?' said Alys.

'Well nothing's perfect,' said Jordan. 'I doubt if I can manage Harry Brag. But perhaps you'll be able to, when you really get going.'

He swept her a bow, and went off singing Avery's old song:

'How hey, it is none lease,
I dare not seyn when she saith Peace!'

Alys was married in the summer after her fifteenth birthday, a year after Jossey had been married to John Lynsy — a fair young man with a job at the king's court, and not totally unlike Sir Herriot Hendy. The two of them came to dance at their sister's wedding.

At Alys's wedding feast Sir Steven's sword from Poitiers, which had pointed at her once, lay on the table with flowers and green leaves all around it; but it wasn't pointing at Alys now.

At the end of the feast, as Roger and Hawkyn tuned up for the dancing, Sir Steven took the sword from the table and put it in Alys's hands.

'For you and your children,' he said. 'Who will all be peace children, after this.'

Alys held the massive sword by the hilt, with its point resting on the ground, and Jordan came and put his hands over hers and helped to hold it steady. Nobody said anything — there had been enough speeches already — but Alys and Jordan kissed as they stood; and the kiss passed around the room — Butler to Castell, and Castell to Butler — as the music began to play.

Author's Note

Harlton, East Hatley and Hungry Hatley (or Hatley St George) are real villages, in Cambridgeshire. In Harlton the faint remains of moats can still be seen in a pasture, and one of these is thought to be the moat that once surrounded a fourteenth-century farmhouse. The area was at one time called 'Butlers Land' or 'Butlers', and appears as 'Lordship Butlers' on a map of 1808; 'Butlers' Spinney' is still called by that name. There was a Peter le Bouteillier owning land in Harlton in the thirteenth century; but I have invented my fourteenth-century Butler family.

There were real Castells in East Hatley, too, but whether they had arrived there in the 1380s is difficult to establish. There is no doubt about the St Georges — they were in Hungry Hatley at that time. They stayed, and the village became known by their name (the earlier name, 'Hungry Hatley', is supposed to have been because of the poor soil there). I have no evidence that Sir Baldwin St George was as bad as I have painted him.

The Great Pestilence (later called the Black Death) devastated England in 1349, and later outbreaks of the same disease (or something very like it) happened in 1361, 1368–9, 1375, 1382 and 1390–91. I have imagined that Thomas died in the 1375 outbreak and Alys and Edward were victims in 1382.

The Peasants' Revolt in 1381 is actual history but I have invented the adventure of Alys and Sir Baldwin St George.

Nobody knows how old the singing-games like *Here comes three Dukes a-riding* are, but there was probably something very like them in fourteenth-century England. Nobody knows, either, whether *Ring-a-ring o' roses* is really connected with the Great Pestilence. We can only guess, and I have guessed that it was.

I don't know whether children were ever exchanged as peace children in England. I heard of this custom being practised by the Sawi people, head-hunters in New Guinea, where 'an infant child from each of two hostile villages was given to the other to be brought up there as a kind of sacred hostage. Peace would be preserved so long as both lived . . . It was enough when violence broke out in the future to lay a hand upon the peace child and so recall the pledge.'

I wondered how this creative idea would work out in England (but it had to be an England before there were adoption laws, and where blood feuds were still known). I wondered even more how the exchanged children would feel about it, when they were old enough to know; and I wrote this book to find out.

FARMINGDALE PUBLIC LIBRARY
3 1736 00122 2753